Fluids

MAY LEITZ

Added Value

I've grown accustomed to titular *author's notes* that don't add much to the overall content of a story. To an extent, I'm asking too much of a writer to provide anything more than what may exist within the confines of a story. That's where the art lives and dies. However, as a frequent reader, I'm familiar with the experience of completing a story and wishing to hear more of that writer's voice elsewhere, even if it breaks the kayfabe of the reality we've enjoyed them within. You complete the final page, then turn back to the beginning of the story to find a forward that you begin reading, assuming that it will somehow spell out the author's intentions and reflections in a way that provides added value. But for some reason, this desire goes unfulfilled, either because there's no value necessary to add or because the author is uncomfortable explaining their magic trick to you. This is an understandable issue I'm now presented with as I'm meant to write an author's note and try to find some added value to store within this essay.

So what am I to do? I know what one desires from a document like this, yet I understand why one shouldn't get to the grit of their story before it's already begun. For someone opening the pages of this story for the first time and reading this, they might get the impression that there is a need to explain myself, and I believe there is.

For one, my story is rough, literally, and in a constructed way. I had no idea what I was doing when I wrote my first book. The dream was so big that I felt like I was climbing a mountain without a path, unsure of how I would even arrive at a book. When you get a book you've completed, you feel the warmth of that success, even if you are unaware of how it functions as a story. We all long for some excuse to feel successful without considering whether we earn it.

I knew I enjoyed writing and could see myself creating fiction, but I didn't expect the writing to leave any impact. I was under the impression that no one in our current year would slow life down enough to read a book, especially considering that I wrote it. But then, when I listed books for sale, I found them leaving the boxes faster than I could keep track of until something like ten thousand copies had been in print. Readers were eager to read my writing and still awaiting the next thing I would write as if this was some kind of planned endeavor.

I never planned to write a second book, nor was the hypothetical third on my hard drive. Writing was all meant to be a challenge. But in doing it, I found a craving for my voice, which I hadn't expected. Looking back on *Fluids*, I see many things I couldn't have predicted. I see a very insecure person trying desperately to find themselves. I'm still exactly like that today, and I have difficulty swallowing my first book's impact on the people who care so deeply for it. I've had so many people ask me questions about it that I had never intended to answer. What is one to do when asked a question about *themselves* for which they don't have an answer? I couldn't tell you.

However, I also see a person who is concerned. Many ask me if the events in Fluids are something true to life. Of course, the answer is no because if the events had occurred in reality, I would likely have been a criminal. But that doesn't mean the events aren't tangentially related to something I found true. The themes are indeed true to me. I don't write characters based on people I know (this part is a lie). But that doesn't mean that the characters in my stories are untrue to life, either. They all come from someone or somewhere because, without them, the truth of the character would lack resonance. So when I refer to myself as *concerned*, I mean as if those people were in front of me and I were documenting their experiences, and I find the things they do or say concerning.

I was on a short road trip with an extended family member when I was twelve. They casually aimed a finger at a bridge overlooking a massive highway and suggested it might be an excellent bridge to jump off. His words were concerning to me at the time, and considering that the man in question is now dead, it worries me even now. There have been plenty of anecdotes like that in my life, not only with friends I've known suggesting the suicide that awaited them some ten years later but also the cruelty admitted so casually. I've heard and ingested the words; thus, *Fluids* cannot be an unexpected response.

I believe that when you're a good listener, people tend to tell you who they are deep down in a manner of speaking. No one is excited to present themselves to you like they would with themselves, but there is occasionally a malaise in their words that appears as a joke or a calm statement. The disregard is often the most shocking part, an inherent aspect of what makes a joke about darkness humorous.

There are moments when intentions become known to those who listen. I've heard these sentiments in my life, and this book is mainly about that. It's about what people can be when indeed left alone with themselves. Sometimes, spoken darkness in a lighthearted tone should be more shocking than it is, but what people can do to themselves and others fascinates me the most. It's all about the moment when a joke ceases to be funny.

Dark humor ceases at action.

There's a great value to literature that one only finds when they're firmly cemented as a fiction writer. The truth is hard to find but easy to see. The truth is plain when you listen, but you can't always know. There's no absolute certainty, even within one's creative confines. Essentially, this is a byproduct of obfuscation. We may not see the truth because it is behind some locked door, and we can't quantify the terror in that room. But we all expect it to be possible.

In this book, I wanted to follow people through those locked doors, where everything they keep to themselves transforms into cruelty. Every one-off joke that sticks in your mind becomes loud and horrific until you realize the joke's contents.

There are only two kinds of humor: a joke about how things are and a joke about how things are absurd. Hyperbole is funny, but only insofar as it isn't entirely based on reality, lest it stop being hyperbole. But the down-and-dirty, garish truth is often amusing as well, and when we laugh at that type of gallows humor, we should pause and ask ourselves if the teller of such a joke is not engaging in hyperbole.

They just might mean it.

PART I: HUNT

1.

Swipe. Swipe. Swipe. Swipe. Swipe. Swipe. Swipe. Swipe.
Left. Left. Left. Left. Right. Left. Right. Left. Left. Left.
Sweating in the dark like a fucking monster. Swipe.
Swipe. Swipe.
Swipe. Swipe. I'm cold. Blanket. Applied blanket for added comfort. And what gets me wet is…
Swipe. Swipe.

Mostly left swipes, unfortunate but typical. Every guy in his twenties looks terrified to be here. Like he's scared that his mom is going to catch him with his dick in his hand. It's sad, honestly, and it kills me every time. It's like looking directly into the void. There's nothing behind their eyes.

Swipe. Swipe. Left. Right.

A girl passes my feed, and I stop to consider.

Her. I can vibe on a 'her.' Being on the matching team sounds pleasant, but unlikely. You get in those situations, and you can feel your pulse rise to such a level that you feel yourself grasping onto life like it's a bomb that's going off in your hands. I like the sensation, but I hate the build-up. I don't want to hook up, but I don't want to earn it. I don't deserve it; I can't afford it.

Swipe. And now I'm just zoning and saying no to everyone, as if what's between my legs is such a prized property. It's not. If my body had value, I wouldn't be treating it like this.

I guess the boredom of this will kill me one day, but today, I'm happily smoking my favorite cigarette. And I'm alone, imagine it. I look down at my ass, and it's genuinely a disgusting shame there isn't someone clawing to get in there.

4

I'm bisexual. Pansexual. I like both. All. I want something, but I like to taste each flavor individually and run it over my tongue with euphoria.

Guy, girl, they. I'm gay for whatever they have, but they only seem to bring around sadness. A body is a body. Equal proportions in today's marketplace of deli meats, and I'm hungry and flexible.

I had a guy back here last night, and while he was able to maintain a hard-on the entire time we had sex, he brought with him this noticeable haste. I can't escape it, like a dance is building in me, and I just want to dance right past him and into whatever crack he was smoking. I want a bump, doctor. I've never seen someone leave so fast.

I mean to say that I'm giddy lately. The mirror disagrees. Yesterday's makeup smeared from having two fingers in my mouth. Don't worry, they weren't mine, Dad. My ass is sore and red under these shorts. I love days when I can just look like shit, but as my dad once told me: "It's better to be ready for an opportunity and not have one than to have an opportunity and not be prepared." I should shower and clean my body. And I should gently remind myself that I shouldn't put anything in my body for the foreseeable future. Maybe give it a rest with that one.

I don't even enjoy penetration. I lie back and watch as if it's a show I'm not allowed to participate in. He thrusts and thrusts and smacks my ass, and I just grin, knowing that he's having fun. Good for him.

Swipe. Swipe. Swipe. I've had this conversation with myself since this morning. I met him on Grindr. What a riot. I met and fucked a *fag* from Grindr. This is fabulous; I should probably put this up on the fridge. There are notches, and then there's this. I'm a genius.

I heard somewhere that when women have sex, they mostly want the story of how the romantic moment unfolded and not the actual physical act itself. While obviously, this is bullshit to anyone that owns a vibrator, I like to think of myself as a tome. I'm a long and sordid history of hands and feet that can't get enough of me.

Swipe. Swipe. Swipe. Boy, the pandemic sure did kill a lot of people. I used to see so many smiling faces, but now no one can stay hard for more than five *minutes*, and asking someone to cum is like asking someone to bury their mother. It's goddamn ridiculous.

I'm going to do it. I can visualize the shower. The water could so efficiently run down my blonde hair and clean this sheen off my skin. I imagine scrubbing myself, shaving. Sometimes I wonder if I'm the one I'm attracted to and not anyone else. This gives dating myself a whole lot more meaning. Maybe I could make it literal.

Sometimes I wonder if I'm that different from the boys these days. I look at myself and look at sad guys on Tinder, and I don't see much difference anymore. It's like a tragic fade has taken over all of us. Dr. Freud would probably tell me that I also haven't been legitimately horny in months and am just beating my pussy to a pulp to spite my depression. Fairly accurate reading there, but my shorts are a lot more comfortable than the possibilities.

People slip and fall in their bathrooms and die all the time. I'm next, you know. It's my destiny as it is yours and as it is all of ours. If you slip and fall and die in the bathroom after reading this, then you're a fucking idiot. I have warned you thoroughly at this point. Anyways, this is my mind. I see death everywhere. What can I say? I'm curious.

I tried to kill myself when I was seventeen, like everyone else. My dad caught me with a knife and laughed at me. I guess he thought I couldn't give myself all the essential cuts because I was a girl. Not realizing that I'd been cutting myself for years: he just never saw my legs. Bitch.

That said, I couldn't give myself the necessary cuts. Instead, I caused a minor bloody accident and felt stupid. It felt good to do something that I knew would break my parents' hearts. I imagine them thinking about me dragging that dirty knife next to my vagina, and it makes me happy. I can't help what it does for me.

There's something so magical and powerful about disappointing your parents.

New Message! Ding! Someone is trying to meet you! Wow!

SUBJECT: **powerful**
SENDER: **Dahliabitch04**

Hey. My name is Dahlia. I wanted to tell you that you seem really cool.

And just like that, I'm wet. The water hits my face, and I feel an overwhelming orgasmic rush. The warmth is the enveloping kind that protects you. Fear of death washes away, and it's replaced with an exuberant new type of sex that only one can have. It cleans and fixes you, putting back together what you try so hard to destroy. It feels so good to put yourself back together, but only because it feels terrific to take yourself apart. I'm like a doll.

The shower gives me all the lubricant I need to scrub my face, my chest, my pussy, my ass, and my legs. I feel such a vibration when I touch my own skin with hot water.

It feels like my whole body is a harp being tuned.

I wish someone would pluck my strings.

I wish I knew how to really pluck those strings myself.

SUBJECT: **Re: powerful**
SENDER: **Lauren666**

Fuck you, you're cool. I'm Lauren.

Listen to this: "The way to my heart is a dark walk in the woods…let's hold hands and talk about Dahmer." Her profile is so fucking edgy I want to die. She makes me feel like I'm in high school.

The first girl I ever had sex with lost her virginity to my fingers and bled down my hand, but she loved grindcore, so we both stared in amazement then talked about how epic it

7

was. I guess I should have clipped my fingernails. Oh, well.

Maybe Dahliabitch04 is like that. Although "Hey, you're cool" is hardly bitch behavior. I feel lied to. She's probably some cottagecore lesbian who is looking for…precisely what I'm looking for.

SUBJECT: **Re: powerful**
SENDER: *Dahliabitch04*

You're so fucking edgy holy shit.

A woman after my own heart. Admittedly, it takes one to know one in my case. I'm a nightmare. I still have my Marilyn Manson poster up from the aughts, but I never took it down more out of laziness than anything. It's the 'Smells Like Children' one that's all green.

Sometimes I wonder if the posters actually fuck up everyone's concentration. I'd have a hard time cumming if a room full of rock stars from the nineties were looking at me. Then again, I look around and can't help but think about all the hotter people I should be fucking. Rockstars don't get distracted by all the shit on your walls. Rockstars don't have shitty breath that infects your mouth for days. Rockstars give you all the drugs and orgasms you want. Look at them. They're practically begging me to join them.

I am really edgy, aren't I? I guess I should accept this. My toenails are black, and I'm twenty-nine. My life is basically over, and this girl is calling me right out.

SUBJECT: **Re: powerful**
SENDER: *Lauren666*

No u. How old are you even? Didn't anyone ever tell you to grow up and get adult hobbies?

That's right. I heard that if you show someone you don't care about them, it has the inverse effect, and they immediately assume you do care. Or maybe it's more about

8

giving people room to doubt. They have to wonder if you're an actual person. You can't assume everyone else is as honest as you are.

SUBJECT: **Re: powerful**
SENDER: *Dahliabitch04*

Video chat.

I sit forward in my pink chair. My wet hair drips on my keyboard but magically never fries it. Shit! I just got out of the shower. I'm fucking naked!

I consider putting clothes on before accepting, but I don't want to risk losing out. So I just jump up and get a shirt on just in time for the video chat to light up on my phone. I clap my thumb to the screen, and my phone heats up with the image of my ceiling.

I look down at my phone, covering my naked legs.

I look down and see a black square where Dahlia is meant to be, and I breathe a sigh of relief. The blackness just sits there, waiting to be disturbed.

I sit and get comfortable at my desk, bringing my knees to my chest, and I brush out my hair with my fingertips. Chewing my lip, I wait for the square to show me an image. I keep waiting. At least I smell better. I wipe under my eyes and there's blackness on my fingers. No matter how hard I clean myself, I find a way to be a mess.

Time begins to become noticeable, and I wonder if it's a technical issue on my end. I reach my arm forward when the call abruptly ends. I grab my phone off the desk and-

SUBJECT: **Re: powerful**
SENDER: *Lauren666*

I'm sorry I couldn't see you. Try calling again?

But as that sends, I get an instant message. My phone heats in my hand and I bask in the LED light. The neon of love piercing through the blue-light filter and somehow still being angelic.

> **Dahliabitch04**: Hey.
> **Lauren666**: What happened?
> **Dahliabitch04**: I'm sorry.
> **Dahliabitch04**: I got nervous, and I couldn't get the courage to turn on my camera.

I suddenly realize that I didn't factor in her appearance in the sheer quantity of people I've looked at today. Her profile *was* vague. It featured images of her at a distance, in a group, or obscured. She is a photographic abstraction. I'm used to people having something to hide. If I'm lucky, it's just a foot fetish or something.

> **Lauren666**: Okay, that's all right. Do you have any pictures of yourself that are current?

She types. Stop. Types. Stop.

I consider the possibility that she isn't who she says she is. But I always remember, in the back of my mind, that whoever someone pretends to be is who they are. The vagueness isn't fear as much as it's authentic to who she is. She doesn't have a personality or an appearance. Not yet. Maybe I have to give her that.

> **Dahliabitch04**: No. I don't have a phone.
> **Lauren666**: Oh, but you have a webcam?
> **Dahliabitch04**: Yeah.
> **Lauren666**: Well, okay, how do I know what you look like then?
> **Dahliabitch04**: There are some pics on my profile.
> **Lauren666**: I can't tell exactly what I'm looking at in them. You're too far away.
> **Dahliabitch04**: I have a problem. I have body dysmorphia.
> **Lauren666**: What's that mean?

Dahliabitch04: My body looks really scary when I look at it, so I can't really take pictures of myself. I only have a couple.

Dahliabitch04: I'm so sorry. I should have mentioned this before the video call. I just wanted to know you were real.

Dahliabitch04: Since the pandemic started, I've been alone, and I haven't had the chance to go out and see anyone at all. I guess I just wanted to know what you looked like in motion.

I stand up, looking at my phone. I've never imagined the way I move to be fascinating. Mostly when I think of myself, I see this big abyss where my past used to be. I think about growing up with my parents and sisters and how that could have formed me into more than this, but here I am. I am *alive*, I guess. The world continues to try harder to push me away from it, but at *least* I'm able to touch it from time to time. What's this bitch's problem?

Voyeurism, that's a new one for me. It's a bland fetish. It's so distant and unemotional and one-sided. I have to pose and lie around so someone I can't see can have a private, comfortable orgasm. I'm more of an uncomfortable, public orgasm kinda person.

One time, a guy I was dating in high school spread my legs apart in a movie theater, got down on his knees, and ate me. I looked at the other couple at the end of the row and laughed, knowing they'd never forget about me. They would never forget the freedom I displayed to them.

Dahliabitch04: I'm sorry. I'll go.

Lauren666: No, wait. Maybe we should start over. I'm still Lauren.

Lauren666: My dad died of Covid two months ago, and I'm not going out or talking to anyone either, and I don't know what to do with myself anymore.

Lauren666: I don't even remember what it's like to date someone. Let alone talk to them. I mostly solve my problems sexually. I don't know.

One day, he wasn't home. I yelled and yelled and yelled, but he never yelled back. He was feeling ill and went out to get a test and never came back. I heard that he died from my aunt. My father didn't even leave me as his emergency contact.

He was just gone one day.

Just like that.

And I'm suddenly scared. It's as if I'm gripped by something beyond myself for the first time. I admitted that I had a problem, and the problem immediately walked into the room to be beside me. For the first time since the end of the world, I'm genuinely terrified, and it's not for my life but for how she responds. It's everything I've fantasized about and feared. Someone else like me.

Dahliabitch04: I'm sorry, Lauren. My name is Dahlia. I'm 28, and I'm...gay.

Lauren666: Like a lesbian?

Dahliabitch04: Yes. I've never been with another girl before, and it's my first time really trying this out, so I'm scared.

Dahliabitch04: I tried to date boys for most of my life, but it never really happened. I dated a couple, but they were rough with me, and I got scared. I didn't want to tell my mom, so I pretended to like the way they treated me.

Dahliabitch04: But then, at the beginning of the pandemic, I told my mom I was gay. I was going to start living my authentic life out in the open with everyone. That was March 2020. Now I see things a lot differently.

I can't come up with anything smart or cute or funny or quippy. My parents always hated me. I feel privileged like that. They hate Lauren. Everyone hates Lauren. A simple fact. That's been my whole life, and somehow that's more normal than losing them. Never having them.

Lauren666: I'm sorry things are so hard right now.
Dahliabitch04: Me too.
Lauren666: Well, I could be your friend.

2.

I'm not so sure I like boys at all anymore. I guess it's not the boys themselves, but their concept. I lie in my bed, and I look at the crowd of rock stars that gather at my bedside every night. I used to see them as a status symbol. Imagine being the girl that is wanted, loved, fucked by these guys.

But when I think about it, I've known guys like this my whole life. I've let guys like these destroy me mentally and physically, and I never complain at all. I just ask myself whose arm I'm attached to. I don't know what's wrong with me.

> *Dahliabitch04*: Who's your favorite serial killer?
> *Lauren666*: Toybox. No, Dahmer, but only because we have to support the gays. Actually...do you know about the Tool Box murders?
> *Dahliabitch04*: No, I only know about Toybox.
> *Lauren666*: Well, besides killing women, they recorded one of the killings, and it's one of the most horrible things you can hear. People listen to it then kill themselves. It's so bad.
> *Dahliabitch04*: Oh my god.
> *Lauren666*: At the end, she's practically begging to die.
> *Lauren666*: Are you still there?

I hate myself.

> *Dahliabitch04*: Yeah. That sounds horrible, but I wanna listen to it now.
> *Lauren666*: Me too. I finally found a transcript! I've been tracking it down for years, but they use it for FBI

desensitization, so it's under wraps.

Dahliabitch04: Oh shit, have you read it?

Lauren666: I have it right here! **{Shady link}**

Lauren666: I'm sorry.

I hate myself.

Dahliabitch04: Wow. This is really fantastic stuff. This sounds like the worst thing in the whole world.

Lauren666: It's definitely one of them.

Dahliabitch04: I think I'm starting to like you.

I stare at the screen, trying to decipher what this phrase means. What does it mean to like someone you've never met? Can she even possibly have feelings that are authentic from a distance?

Lauren666: I like you too.

I have no idea what she looks like.

Dahliabitch04: I really want to hear your voice.

Lauren666: I really want to see your face. Is it horrible?

Dahliabitch04: I don't know. I don't really remember what I'm supposed to look like.

I want to be angry about this. I want to say, "No! If we're going down this road, I have to know!" But I can't be upset about this because it's true of me too. I wonder if the last few months of meaningless sex were only so I could remember my value or beauty or...something. I wonder if the last few months of meaningless sex were leading me to her. Of course, this is true. I am here.

Lauren666: I don't remember what I look like either. Maybe we can both just be faceless, anon.

Dahliabitch04: I think you're beautiful.

I don't have any recent pictures on my profile because I haven't taken any in months. It feels weird to hear that I'm beautiful when my images aren't even me anymore, and there doesn't seem to be any hope for the future of my appearance. I haven't eaten well in months, and my face is so sullen and tired. Maybe I'm ugly now, and she's going to find out somehow.

I remember our short video call.

Lauren666: Can we talk? I just...I need something. I know the appearance thing is hard nowadays, but surely, we can talk, right?
Lauren666: If I could hear you, I think I'd feel all better.

A few minutes pass.
The silence always tells me Dahlia is thinking.
She's thinking about me. Even if I'm no one to her, she still thinks about me.

Dahliabitch04: I'm scared.
Lauren666: Of me?
Dahliabitch04: Yes.
Lauren666: I don't want to pressure you. It's just something I need.

I'm sorry, Dahlia. I'm stuck in the fetal position on my bed with my phone close enough to my face to feel its heat. I'm the bitch here. The world isn't like it used to be, and asking for it to be the same is asking for suffering. The time of appearances is truly over. We're only souls now.

Dahliabitch04: Okay.
Lauren666: Okay?
Dahliabitch04: Yeah, we can do it.

I feel the immediate need to puke rise in my throat, and I run from the room. I grab my bong and grinder and lie on the floor of the bathroom, trying to catch my breath. I'm able to pull myself together long enough to build a bowl of weed, and I heat it up and inhale the vapors. It fills me with brief anxiety and uncertainty. I blink furiously and remember to push down the urge to cough. I exhale, and my stomach pressure gives way, and I burp. My stomach flattens.

Lauren666: Call whenever you're ready.

I retch over the toilet and heave nothing. I look in, disappointed. Usually, if my body doesn't produce something when I retch, it won't stop until something comes out. I decide that it's the right time to push myself to power through. I force myself to vomit twice. After that, I'm able to relax slightly. The vomit is mostly acid that burns my throat as it exits. I haven't eaten since yesterday. Since meeting Dahlia, I haven't felt an ounce of hunger or thirst.

Part of me wonders if I'm feeding off her energy alone.

I remember watching a video about Breatharians, people who eat only through breathing. The irony is that most of them don't actually take it seriously, but those that do very quickly decay and die.

Dahliabitch04: Calling.

I hold my phone with one hand and my hair with the other. I pull it behind my shoulders, careful not to get it stuck on my lips, still covered in some mysterious phlegm. It rings.

"Hello?" I answer, quietly and casually, as if she's caught me playing video games and not vomiting. She doesn't respond immediately. The silence is palpable in a way that eats inside me. I feel the retching coming again but can stifle it. I hover my finger over the mute key.

"Dahlia?" I say. "I'm really nervous about talking to you too."

I mute my phone with swiftness and retch into the toilet again. Tears start streaming down my face. An involuntary reaction. Humans are just a tube, after all. Just a tube.

"Meow," Dahlia allows. Her voice is immediately

confusing to my whole body. I'm unable to understand her inflection. But the sound coming out of the phone is life. Life is something I sorely miss and barely understand.

"Meow," I toss back.

"Meow."

"Meow."

It's a standoff. But with every word Dahlia says, I can hear her more and more. It's as if the ghost of a sad cat possessed my phone.

"Dahlia?"

"Meow?" she calls back.

"Is this you or a cat that I've accidentally called?" I consider that jokes might lubricate an actual conversation.

There's no response.

"...Okay, I've tried really hard up to this point, but if you aren't willing to even speak to me-"

"I'm sorry. I'm just petrified. I've never been this scared before," she squeaks out before returning to silence. I haven't ever been this scared, either. I've never vomited from the anticipation of meeting someone before, but here I am. Still, there's immediate relief in her voice. It's as if I'm comforted by a mother, not mine but someone's.

"Do you ever feel like…you do something, and you're terrified, but then afterward you're glad you did it, and you feel better?" I let it slip and immediately feel regret. "Just in general..."

"I know that feeling," she mutters. Dahlia sounds like a sad person who secretly wants to be satisfied. She comes across as the kind of person who could have a happy disposition if she ever looked up from the floor. She's just like me. We need to start looking at each other and not at the ground, and then we'll make it.

"Ya know what I think, Dahlia?" I cough out with a half laugh and half throat pain. "I think we need each other."

There's silence over the phone, but I imagine she's smiling. Maybe she's crying. Perhaps this is the moment for her when she feels less alone and accepts that her life can get better if only she lets me into it.

18

But then she says, "You do?"

"I don't know what it is about you, but I want to be your best friend in the whole world. I want to take you to Disneyland and ride in those little teacups. I want to go to the beach with you and drink Coronas. I want to do drugs with you. Do you like drugs?" I shout. "I want to introduce you to my mom. Not, like, to get her approval, but to rub it in her stupid face. I want to be your best friend." I mute the phone and vomit solid waste this time. Thank God. Thank heaven and all that's holy. Allah Akbar.

I imagined her moved and shaken on her foundations. I can see her legs giving out with love and bravery.

"But we just met. I barely know you."

I break my concentration and realize I'm clutching my phone with all my might. I'm lying on the ground now in a pool of sweat. I realize now just how high I am on bong rips. My lungs feel light as air, but two demonic claws grip my heart and pull me back to earth with a thud. I collapse in on myself.

I hear the sound of a mechanical keyboard for a gaming PC. All at once, something ugly dawns on me. My imagination's getting away from me, I made a closet case gamer from the internet into something bigger. I don't even know her. I'm alone.

"You're right. I'm sorry." I exhale, and all the stress of my failure comes with it, and tears well up and release. My lips and mouth burn. My lungs burn. My throat burns. I imagine myself engulfed in flames and burning alive. It's probably like this, but shorter.

"I should go," I say. "I hope things get better for you."

And then I let go. Then the glass top skin sensor button presses, and she's gone. My thumb hurts from the act.

My body relaxes, and the whole of me separates from the physical. I lie myself down in the spiritual dimension for a moment and catch my psychic breath. She could be anyone. Dahlia could be anyone, and I could be anyone. No one is anyone anymore. And if anyone was someone, would we all collectively hate them? Is there a collective anymore?

I miss her.

Some kind of loss engulfs me, and I'm aware of just how lonely my evening was. Part of me knows that I do this so I don't have to tolerate the silence of my dad's absence. I understand that it's self-destructive, but I forgot how not to self-destruct.

I flush the toilet and leave the bathroom to die. Next stop, bed. I land and scream bloody murder into the bedsheets. The scream rattles the soft cushion and my stomach below. I don't even know what I want. I don't know what any of this is about. What is wrong with me anymore?

3.

Swipe. Swipe. Swipe. Swipe. Swipe.
Right. Right. Right. Right. Right.
I should shower. Swipe. Right. Right.
Put me back together.
God, I *need* a boyfriend.

Just someone to tell me what to do all the time. Order me around. Make me cry for tangible reasons that have nothing to do with the world itself. Fuck. I understand why Virginia Woolf walked into the sea. I want to walk into the sea.

I should. I should find a bunch of rocks and fill the pockets of my cardigan and see how long I can swim. God, the water sounds fine.

Shower. Washing my hair and rinsing my hair and washing my face, and why am I washing at all? For whom? Myself? I'm so tired of the moments I see myself followed quickly by myself turning into a shapeless mass. Where am I anymore? Am I dead? Did I die, and is this all that's left of me now? I want to die, but I think I'm already dead.

I throw a towel on my hair, and I brush the horrible taste out of my teeth. My phone lights up. I grip the toothbrush between my teeth and look down.

Dahliabitch04: Hey, what's your day looking like?

I feel an immediate rush, and then anger. The absolute gall of this bitch to text me this shit after that shit.

Lauren666: I don't know.

I don't. I never do. What are the days? My dad is haunting

my house now. I find myself in the kitchen saying something to him about the house needing repairs, and I have the whole conversation with him before realizing he was never there. He was never there to begin with. I hated him. He was such a bastard, but now, when I say words out loud, they bounce off the walls and back into my own ears. I can be my own best friend now. I don't need a friend anymore; I have my ghost dad and me.

I want to be relieved that I don't have to hate him anymore.

I want to be happy that he's gone.

But I'm just angry that he isn't here.

Dahliabitch04: We could play games together. Do you have a Steam account?

Lauren666: I don't want to talk to you anymore.

Dahliabitch04: What, why?

Lauren666: You make me sick to talk to. I speak to you, and I feel like I'm going to die. It feels like something is coming to kill me, and when I look at my phone, I should see cute animals and happy thoughts, but no, I just see you, and I don't even know what you look like. It's such bullshit.

Lauren666: You're going to make me destroy myself, I swear.

Dahliabitch04: I took a picture with my webcam…

I sit up straight. My hair is wet, and it drips on my keyboard. Luckily I don't die this time, but I know one day the fates will find me. I blink my eyes until I find the mental dexterity to process her appearance.

Lauren666: Are you going to send it to me?

Dahliabitch04: Yeah. Uhm. We should be friends. I just have never had a friend before. *{Attachment}*

I stare in amazement for a minute. I reach for my bong. I load the bowl, ignite the lighter, press my face to the hole and suck hard. I take the rip and exhale myself out through my nose. I float around the room and over the picture of Dahlia, examining every detail. There she is. She's amazing. She's the most beautiful woman I've ever seen. She might as well be the only woman I've ever seen. She practically invented femininity. She's everything I wish I was myself. She's more powerful than I could possibly have imagined. I feel my terror double.

She's a brunette. Her hair is tied back and clearly hasn't been cut in ages. She wears a dress that looks like a picnic table but has a homely charm that makes her feel like someone from a southern romance story. I can see her hands around my waist. I can see my fingers finding their way through her fingers. I wish I could hold her.

Dahliabitch04: I'm sorry.

I stare at the message and know I have to save her, but I cannot figure out how. Apologizing for such beauty is baffling, and it upsets my high brain. I fidget and squirm and squint, and I hate it more and more.

Dahliabitch04: My whole life, I've had a hard time making friends, and I never heard anyone talk to anyone like you spoke to me. Outside of the movies.
Lauren666: You're beautiful.

I'm gripping my hair and trying desperately not to push the mental button that tears it out of my head, making me unfuckable.

Dahliabitch04: Meow?
Lauren666: Is that really you?
Dahliabitch04: Yes, I took that this morning. Just for you.
Lauren666: I don't know what to say.
Dahliabitch04: Neither do I.

It's happening, and I'm hopeless. It's happening, and I'm useless.

Lauren666: I think I'm a lesbian.
Lauren666: I think I've always been a lesbian, but for some reason, you showed me that just now. I don't think I ever want to be with a man again.
Dahliabitch04: Oh. Lauren, that's a lot.

My eyes drift around the room and find all the posters of rockstars that I know deep down would never give me the love I want. They'd want me to lie down and show no resistance, even when they hurt me. They don't want to be next to me; they want me behind closed doors. They aren't even real.

None of these men look like this anymore. They never looked like this. They were this for a second when a cameraman painted them with light, but then they returned to a quiet state of nothingness.

Lauren666: If I'm not a lesbian, then there's something wrong with me. Maybe I have some kind of problem with my health, but I get so scared whenever I think about you.
Dahliabitch04: Me too.
Lauren666: Why do you get scared?
Dahliabitch04: Because you feel like a nuclear bomb. You feel like the kind of person that is really close to doing something really awful.
Dahliabitch04: I once knew a guy who was at a gay club when Jeffrey Dahmer was there, but Jeff didn't pick him. He was too ugly for the serial killer. Can you believe that?
Dahliabitch04: He tells everyone that he danced with Dahmer. You feel like that to me. Talking to you feels like dancing with Dahmer.

I take a glance out my window, half-obscured by a brick wall. The skyline is a pure grey with nothing for miles

24

around. I remember those ads from the aughts about cyberbullying and how, if someone is mean to you online, you should just unplug your computer. But what do you do when your online life follows you around? What if every device in your house reminds you that you have a new message from the girl that wants to hatefuck you? I wouldn't want to live in that house, but here we are.

Lauren666: I don't like this.
Lauren666: What does that even mean? Like, you don't know me well enough to say something so fucking absurd! I keep reading it to see if you were joking, but no... you're fucking serious.
Lauren666: I don't understand.
Dahliabitch04: I just meant that like...you're cool, and I want to hang out with you. Like...you seem like my kind of crazy, and I like crazy.
Lauren666: Isn't that kind of a shitty thing to call someone? You can't just say I'm crazy.
Dahliabitch04: Well, but...come on.
Lauren666: Wtf does that mean?
Dahliabitch04: Fine.

I hate myself. I look out the window into the abyss and know it won't help me. I look at the ceiling and find no answers there. The posters sit rotting on the walls.

Lauren666: I'm probably defensive. I do that sometimes. My ex-girlfriend used to tell me that I got defensive really quickly and then wouldn't listen. So... I'm listening.
Dahliabitch04: I just like you.
Lauren666: I like you.
Dahliabitch04: Will you be my girlfriend?
Lauren666: Yes.

The impulse took over. I am no longer Lauren, but some greater Lauren. Bigger Lauren. Lauren smokes the bowl and feels more prominent, even though she's making a mistake.

She's never been in an online relationship, and she's ready for it to suck dick.

It's going to suck dick.

I'm going to regret this.

I wish my dad was here.

He wouldn't support me for shit. What am I talking about? I should go down to the kitchen and see if he's around.

It's the evening, and I can already feel a stormy night gripping the house. The kitchen is musty and cold. I pour myself a glass of cold purified water and joke to myself about it extending my lifetime. Yummy.

"Dad, I have a new girlfriend," I proclaim into the emptiness. "She's from the internet."

The emptiness looks back but remains quiet.

4.

It's morning, and I'm gay. It's noon, and I'm still gay. I have a feeling when it gets to be evening, I'm still going to be gay. Dahlia is my girlfriend. I'm taking a shower, and Dahlia is my girlfriend. I don't know her eye color or her last name or where she lives or if she drives or…

> *Dahliabitch04*: I'm from Oklahoma. I live in a small town called Moore. It's in the center of the state. I'm on a 15-acre farm, but no one here grows anything. We had a goat once.
>
> *Lauren666*: Oh my god, you live on a fucking farm?
>
> *Dahliabitch04*: It's not much of a farm, but I live on land.
>
> *Lauren666*: I'm not too far from you, only a couple of hours' drive.
>
> *Lauren666*: My dad used to get in fights with my mom, and then we would drive through the country all day, so I'm kind of used to long drives.

Then I wait. I wait and wait and wait. I think about typing more, but then I delete it and feel stupid.

After a couple of hours, I accept she won't be responding. I worry I scared her off or put too much on her at once. I think about apologizing but consider that my constant apologies might be more annoying, so I resign myself to doing nothing.

I read about a cult of people that gave women abortions against their wills. I learn about a castle in Mexico where they torture prisoners so bad that they have to drown out the screams with pop music. Imagine being tortured to death, but you can't get away from Lady Gaga. She will be your personal spiritual guide through the worst moments of your life.

I learn that there are ISIS beheading videos in 4K that you can stream online.

I learn that a brick fell off a truck on the highway and decapitated a woman while her family was shooting a home movie.

I learn that if you smoke enough DMT, you can break through to a dimension of wizards and elf people that teach how to control reality.

I realize that AI will destroy us if it hasn't already started to.

I learn that there's a fetish online for bald men to stick their heads in women's vaginas.

Lauren666: We don't have to meet up. I'm sorry if I'm going too fast. I'm just really excited about you. I know it's not safe to meet up. We could get each other sick. I just want to know you better, and I don't want to wait. I've sat in my house and felt alone for months, and I need…I don't want to wait to get to know you.

And then I resign myself to bed. Goodnight bullshit, smell ya later. I am considering trying to find someone new again. I'm thinking about getting railed. I'm thinking about getting fucked, but it makes me feel ill. Why does it feel so wrong now?

My phone lights up my room's darkness, and suddenly I'm wide awake again.

Dahliabitch04: I have to be honest with you entirely if we're going to be close, and I'm sorry to do this to you now after everything that's happened. There's a lot. Uhm. I feel so bad for keeping this from you, but in my perfect world, it doesn't matter. In a just world, it wouldn't matter, but that's not our world. We're in a world where people are cruel, and you might also be cruel...I don't know. I don't know yet.

Dahliabitch04: But liking you is the biggest mistake I could make because one day you'll want to meet me and one day you'll want to spend time with me in my life and...my life isn't good. My life isn't something anyone would call normal. I don't want to scare you off, but if we're ever going to be close, you have to know.

Dahlia is typing... Dahlia is typing...

Dahliabitch04: I'm transgender. I live away from most other people because going out is dangerous where I live. I used to go to a support group with a girl named Charlie, and she was murdered here. The locals don't like gays of any kind, and I know you aren't like me...But I'm petrified of the people here. And I'm scared to death of you. I've just never felt like this before, and I don't want to ruin it by being different somehow.

Dahliabitch04: I still have my...parts. I don't hate them, but I don't use them, and they make me uncomfortable to think about. I understand if you'd never want to be intimate with me for this reason.

Dahliabitch04: I used to think that I was kind of like a doll. When I was a kid, I'd imagine myself taken apart like a puzzle and rearranged into a different thing altogether. If I just removed a bit of myself and mixed the remaining pieces, maybe I could fit together in a way that I never felt I could. Or I might not get rearranged at all. Just taken apart piece by piece and left in a metal drum. Either way, I wish I could take parts of myself away and make this all more manageable, but I can't.

The light of my phone keeps breaking through the darkness, each piece of information more illuminating than the last.

Lauren666: So, the pictures and the call.

Dahliabitch04: Yeah, I was scared you'd notice.

Lauren666: I've never been with someone like you before.

Dahliabitch04: Neither have I.

Something breaks like a firecracker in my lower abdomen, like a pill-taking effect. Suddenly my pelvis is awry with sensation. I press my fingers on my thighs, and the feeling is overwhelming. I think about Dahlia holding my hair and gripping my neck with her teeth like I'm her prey. I think about her breaking me apart like so many have failed to do. I'm not afraid of her now. I'm mesmerized by the possibilities.

Lauren666: I'm okay with that. None of that bothers me at all.

Dahliabitch04: ...Really?

Lauren666: I'm nervous about asking questions, but I feel like I'm going to need to know some things to adapt to your needs.

Dahliabitch04: Maybe we should talk about this later. I need to process this.

And then Dahliabitch04 goes *offline*.

I say, "Okay, fine," but in my mind, I'm thinking about her hands wrapped around my waist. I've never considered what it would be like to have sex with a trans woman. She might prefer not to do things in a penetrative fashion. But the thought of her writhing underneath me still takes me to the same place. A better place. Suddenly, I find all this even hotter.

Saying goodnight is no longer what I want. It takes everything in me not to immediately revert to old habits, yesterday's practices.

I could make that drive right now. I have no reason not to. I know that town. I could make that drive. But why? For what? Do I really have so little to live for as to pack up and leave my dad? He needs me here. He needs me to take care of his house while it dies along with him.

There's no good reason not to drive three and a half hours to Moore, Oklahoma right now to see this poor, poor girl. This poor girl whose soft legs could wrap so gently around mine. What does a girl's breath feel like? What does a girl's sweat smell like? I can't remember.

5.

Switching. Switching. Switching. Switching.

There's no good radio station in the mountains. Pathetic fucking mountains too. They're small and puny, yet they catch the radio signal and fuck it up. And you only wish for the radio on nights like this, right when no radio signal is available.

Switching. Switching. Switching.

I'm driving ninety-five miles an hour down the road because there's never a cop here for a hundred miles, and I like a girl. I won't be slowing down, but some music would help.

What the fuck can I possibly say when I get there? Hey, I know you're sleeping and are clearly uncomfortable with too much too fast, but I drove across the state to see you tonight in the middle of the night, three days after we met. I'm sure she won't have any issues with that. I know it's a bad idea, but it's the only idea. If I stay in the house, I'm going to join Dad. I'll sit there on the ground and find the essential spots and make those necessary cuts. But at least back there, I'm in control.

Two hours left, and I rub my eyes because I'm tired. It occurs to me it might be best to wait until morning to do my surprise visit. I don't know Dahlia's address, but I know enough to get there by morning. I can be the first thing she sees. I can prove her wrong, I can take her out and show her off and hold her hand, and there won't be anyone around to give us trouble. I can walk her around, and she will feel so loved at my side.

Sometimes change hurts us. It asks us to do more than we feasibly can, and so it stretches us like a muscle. Growth

32

is painful in the same way decay is. We all think it's impossible to decay when it's only the natural growth process in reverse. We've already been through it. We're all begging for that change, but none of us can do it for ourselves, and it always hurts. She will probably be resistant, but she'll come around and see it my way after some time. So many people live their lives to prevent growth and decay, but I'm here to help everyone embrace it.

I should stop at a diner and give myself a rest and some coffee before my big adventure. The more I think about it, the hungrier I get. Food and coffee are just what I need, and they'll give me all the time in the world to think and plan.

I drive for about ten miles before I see a diner and pull into a spot. I check my phone, and the screen blinds me in the dark car. She hasn't messaged me back, which makes me imagine her like a child asleep in bed. It makes me feel a motherly protectiveness towards her. She's precious. Goodnight, sweet angel. Big day tomorrow.

I sit down, and a lady brings me coffee, but I hardly notice. I wonder if Dahlia's going to be wearing a picnic table dress like in the picture. I wonder if she's going to kiss me.

When I was in high school, I met this girl online, and we went to a bridge by her house, and she kissed me on that cute little bridge. I took that as a cue to have sex with her right there in the park. We both ended up with bloody knees from fucking on the concrete ground under the bridge. I was so busy fucking her I didn't even notice that a piece of glass had entered my knee. When I pulled it out, it sprayed blood all over her Taylor Swift t-shirt. Thinking about that always makes me flutter a little.

I won't make such a mistake with Dahlia. If she kisses me, I'll just enjoy the kiss itself. I won't take any more than that, and I won't push her in any direction.

"Late night drive?" the waitress asks, as if I've materialized here and my presence requires an explanation.

"Yeah, I'm going to see my girlfriend." It feels good to say. It feels authentic and proud, and unstoppable. I'm powerful.

"Girlfriend?" she says while folding a napkin and placing silverware precisely between the folds. "She sounds like a lucky woman."

"She's…" I don't know what to say or how to explain myself to her. I'm not sure that I even need to. Instead, I just smile. I could tell her to fuck off, and it wouldn't make even a slight difference. "I met her online."

"Aww! That's so sweet!" she exclaims. "My brother met his wife on online dating, and I'm just always so happy to hear people find love."

Love. How many days are meant to pass before one allows themselves permission to feel the love?

"True love is hard to find these days…" she trails away.

I sip the blackness, and it fills my mouth with sweet poison. I heard once that morgue workers can always tell which corpses drank a lot of coffee because their organs have a putrid smell. Mine are going to rot, and I'm okay with that. I check my handbag for cigarettes and find a pack with three. One for me now, two for Dahlia and me to share later on when the time is right.

"Can I smoke in here?" I pop the cigarette in my mouth and flick the lighter.

"Well, it's against state regulation, but no one's ever here on account of Covid, so I don't really mind," she says. She has kind grey eyes, like her abyss is somehow brighter than mine and everyone else's. She's like a goddess presiding over my evening. She could grant all my wishes. Oh, how I wish Dahlia was as into me as I am into her. I pull on the cigarette, and it fills me with profound completion.

"Thank you," I say. "I needed that."

6.

It's six in the morning, and I'm sitting in my car at a crossroads with fresh coffee. I have a giant smile on my face because I know the woman I love is in this town, and nothing on Earth can stop me from seeing her today. Nothing.

I check my phone, but there's still nothing. Dahlia seems to sleep like an average person, which she and I will never have in common. I know that as soon as she wakes up and texts me, I will begin retching and hissing and yowling and screeching and vomiting all over the place like a diseased cat. I know this is my future, yet I drink the coffee, and it makes me excited. There's a fine line between excitement and terror, and I'm walking that line.

I park my car on the side of the road by a field, and I get out. It's time to stretch my legs and get used to the idea of Oklahoma. I've never spent significant time here on foot, only driving through. The houses look old but are still on the brink of being suburban. There's usually a main house, a vast section of land, and some extravagant barn. In the more affluent areas, these houses are massive, impressive, and bourgeois. But in the poor neighborhoods, you're inches from the *Texas Chain Saw Massacre.*

You can only imagine some of those barns filled with the corpses of dead teenagers from the local high school. I suspect that every small town has an open secret about the one creepy guy that loves to kill drifters. I'm a drifter, but I could only be so lucky.

I've never killed anyone, but part of me has always been curious. Sometimes, when I look at crime scene photos, I feel the impulse to lie down next to the poor, mangled person. I feel a call to action when I see a dead body. I want to help. I know helping doesn't mean giving them life. It means making them more comfortable with death. We're all envious of the dead.

But the thought of the local high school getting torn apart slowly just fills me with glee. All those poor cheerleaders who are definitely not gay being forced to die right next to the other girls they've always wanted to fuck. I imagine myself placing them together in a loving embrace right as their souls leave and it's so beautiful my eyes water.

I put my phone on vibrate and hope for a signal, which is difficult in this area of the country. Nevertheless, I should feel my phone buzz as soon as I get a signal and Dahlia wakes up. Until then, I have one task: learn about Oklahoma. I feel like I'm going to be spending a lot of time here, so it makes sense to learn as much as I can.

My mom once told me that if you wore a hat in Oklahoma and went into a bar, some guy would inevitably call you a fag and beat the shit out of you. For a hat? Yes, for wearing a hat, she would say before laying some other horrible truth on me. I feared my own lesbianism for the longest time because she told me things when I was young and impressionable. Now I'm a fucking mess, and she can't possibly wonder why. That's how Jeffrey Dahmer's parents must feel too.

I take a walk down a country road. On either side of me, the houses are lined with life. It's as if Covid never hit here, and if it did, no one was affected. I guess everyone had so much fucking space they didn't need any extra distance.

It's quiet, and I mean silent. I don't remember the last time I heard pure silence and pure peace. I smell the air, the oxygen. I taste the sweet air, and it feels more like home than I've ever felt. I guess this is her power. This is how I know she's close by. There's a sweetness in the air that could only belong to her.

Maybe if I keep walking, I'll run into her house. I'll knock on her door. I can imagine her sleepy eyes bewildered when she realizes her new girlfriend drove all the way to see her and wasn't even afraid. Maybe she'll hug me and cry and hold me. We'll have each other. We'll lie in her bed, growing together. We'll be like a massive amoeba that grows and grows, completing itself but dooming the world.

Something is compelling here. Call it what you like, but I feel guided now, like the ground will come up and carry me. It's taking me right where I need to be, and I shouldn't get in the way of that process. I'm being brought home by something larger than myself, and finally I can breathe.

I don't feel my dad looking over my shoulder anymore.

It's only me.

I'm alone.

All at once, I see a truck driving down the street. It's dawn, so vision is difficult on such flat land, but I can see that the pickup is white. It's going fast, but still slow enough to come to a near stop when passing me.

The truck slows long enough for a window to come down.

A window comes down just in time for the voice inside the car to yell.

All of this takes long enough for me to hear the words "Fuck off, dyke!" before the truck drives off at the speed of light.

Something grips me again, and I realize where I am and what I'm doing.

Oh my God, I drove to Dahlia's hometown.

Oh my God, I'm in Oklahoma.

Oh my God, I'm alone.

Oh my God, my dad is dead and will never come back.

Oh my God, I'm a lesbian, and I always have been.

Oh my God, I'm a lesbian who drove to Oklahoma into the middle of a small town and didn't consider the possible dangers, and the only person I can call is the very person who would be horrified if she found out I drove here.

Oh my God, I need to go home.

Back in the car and I realize the lack of marijuana in my blood is making me paranoid. A large amount of coffee is making me paranoid. The strange events of the day and the ambiguity of the place are bothering me. Nothing more than that. Nevertheless, I realize now what a mistake I'm making.

For one, if I were her, and I woke up to a girl at my doorstep…Well, I guess I'd probably fuck her. Yes. I would. If a strange girl showed up at my door, I'd be overjoyed.

Looking around, I remember the truth of the situation. This isn't home. This is a rescue mission. She said her life fucking sucks, and now I understand. I can get her out of here. I can. I know I can.

I have at least enough money for a tank of gas back home. We can stay at my haunted house and take care of it.

It'll be perfect.

I have to save Dahlia.

I wish someone would have saved me.

I check my phone, and it's only been thirty minutes, and she still hasn't texted me. It is nearly seven in the morning, so I can't expect her to be too active. Even if she is awake, she's going to need coffee or tea and some kind of pick me up before immediately hopping on her computer. I sip my coffee and feel its sweet anxiety. Oh my God, I'm going to be sick. I can't back down from this. I have to actually commit to this. I can't fail anymore. This is what being gay is. I can't fail at being what I clearly am, and this is natural for me. This is natural.

I puke coffee out my car window all down the side of my shitty Honda. It bothers me, but at the same time, I'm beginning to call the puking home as well.

I'm never going to understand this girl's effect on my stomach. Even vomiting makes me happy because I'm vomiting for her. I never vomited for a boy except for the time some guy jammed his cock too far into the back of my throat, and I spat bile all over his stomach. The lurching was hilarious in hindsight.

Vomiting is something that I view as hideously unpleasant but instantly freeing. We are all just tubes, after all. Clearing out my tube satisfies the part of me that has a hard time swallowing anything. It's the reason I can't be straight. I lived in fear of vomiting on another dude's dick ever since that happened, and now a girl can make me gag by existing.

But as I lurch outside the car and give my breakfast to the birds to eat, I can't help but feel happy to have had her spirit inside me at all. I've never felt so complete.

7.

It isn't until about two in the afternoon when she texts me. I promised myself I'd make her text me first today, but I started really regretting it around noon. I was afraid to walk around because I didn't want to deal with more of the area's hospitality. I drank so much coffee that I began to feel really ill and carried it around with me for hours before finally depositing the remaining contents of my stomach on the pavement of one of the few roads in town.

All the businesses are closed, except for the gas station. I found a spot in the parking lot and made that my home base.

Dahliabitch04: Baby, I had a dream about you!

Lauren666: You did? What did you dream about??

Dahliabitch04: I dreamed about you. I guess it was a silly thing, but I dreamed about a bridge. Just a cute bridge.

Dahliabitch04: And I was standing on it waiting in the darkness. I stayed there for the whole dream. I thought I'd never stop waiting.

Dahliabitch04: Then finally, out of the mist...you joined me on the bridge. And I was scared of you because you crept out of the darkness like you were going to rob me or attack me, but I caught you! And then it was you.

Dahliabitch04: When you got caught, you backed down and disappeared into the dark where you came from. But when you left, I felt forlorn. I wanted to talk to you. So I decided to wait for you to come back. And I woke up waiting.

If only Dahlia knew how much I can relate. I'm barely keeping things together at this point. I need a place out of the sun and with A/C that actually works. Water, I need water. But there are only so many times you can re-enter the same gas station before they wonder if you're going to rob them.

> *Lauren666*: That's so sweet. Wow. I really like that.
> *Dahliabitch04*: I think it's kind of sad now that I type it all out.
> *Lauren666*: :(why sad? It sounds like you like me!
> *Dahliabitch04*: I guess I wish you would have stayed. I didn't want to be afraid of you. I just couldn't help it. Sometimes other people are scary even when they don't mean harm. And sometimes, the most innocent people are the worst and do the most damage.
> *Dahliabitch04*: I guess I wish I would have given you a chance.

At this point, the last couple of days overwhelm me, and my sexual urges become difficult to contain. I am in Dahlia's hometown, and if she wanted to give me a chance, she could. I rub my pussy above my jeans. I didn't consider what I was wearing when I left, and now she might see me soon. Fuck. I couldn't possibly care. I have euphoria pouring between my fingers.

The thought of her fingers crawling inside me, in between mine, feels like destiny. My body heaves with pleasure. I sit in my car by the roadside, barely holding myself together. I feel a bullet form in between my legs, and I know I have to fire it as soon as possible. But I have priorities. It's vital that I don't leave her to deal with this alone.

Nevertheless, I shove one hand into my pants, cup my clitoris between two fingers, and cradle it. I shriek with pleasure and, with my available hand, grab my phone.

> *Lauren666*: I have a secret.

I'm going to fucking explode. I know that if Dahlia were

here, this would just blow her mind. I wish I was there to blow her mind. I could fuck her. I could fuck her right now. I could drive to her house right now and fuck her. Oh God, I'm gonna fucking puke, dude.

I think her fingers are the only ones I want to interact with my tube anymore. Even if it's just my throat.

> ***Dahliabitch04***: Meow? A secret?
> ***Dahliabitch04***: Will you tell me your secret?

I want to. I want to tell Dahlia my secret so bad, but my other secret prevents my hand from even gripping the phone. I feel the moisture trickle between my ass, and it somehow makes me gush. I want her so bad I can barely stand it. And I could fuck her. Like the girl on the bridge. I wouldn't even care if my knees got bloody and the ground got sharp. It would take everything in me to stop from immediately devouring her. But I have to. I can't fuck her. I can't. I said I wouldn't. I said she was special. She is special. I wouldn't have come all this way for someone who wasn't unique. I can't let this happen. Fuck.

> ***Lauren666***: I did something really, really bad.

I decide at this moment that if I don't cum, then for the rest of the day, I'm going to act ridiculous. I won't be able to hold myself together. If I don't cum soon, I'm going to do something awful to her and fuck up the best relationship of my life. We're talking about love here. If I drop the ball on this, I'll be the biggest failure.

> ***Dahliabitch04***: What did you do?
> ***Dahliabitch04***: Lauren, what's going on?
> ***Dahliabitch04***: Lauren?
> ***Dahliabitch04***: Lauren, you're scaring me.

I splay my legs apart and imagine her hand reaching up my body, gripping my throat and choking me until I can't breathe. When I open my eyes, I find my hand around my own neck. Grabbing like mad, I rub the hood of my clit and exhale the remaining contents of my lungs. I grip hard on my neck, so no matter what I do, I can't get another breath of air. As soon as I start to see black blobs in my vision, I let go, and all at once, I cum hard in the driver's seat.

I gasp for air and gasp and gasp and gasp. I gasp so hard that my lungs fill with pain, no doubt from the cigarettes and vomiting. My pelvis thrashes and thrashes, and I feel myself nearly urinate from the intensity. I grip the steering wheel and feel it lock from my jerking. I quietly thank God that there are no other cars in the parking lot.

I finally get my heart rate down and notice how green it is outside my windows. It's beautiful, like nothing I've ever seen. I roll my window down and enjoy the silence and the oxygen. It's a shame this place is owned by bastards because it would be a beautiful place to call home.

This is a rescue mission.

Lauren666: Sorry, I was in the middle of something. I didn't do anything too crazy, don't worry. I just caught a wild hair last night, and I remembered that my dad used to drive us through Moore, Oklahoma, all the time, so I got curious if I remembered how to go there.

Lauren666: Well, I drove and drove all night, and I remembered the way, and then when I looked up, I realized I was in Moore. So I don't know how to say this, but I'm here. I'm parked next to a cornfield at a gas station.

I hate myself. I desperately search the car for anything to get rid of the moisture collecting on my butt. When I move, a mixture of sweat and cum squelches, and I can feel it chafing my skin.

Dahliabitch04 is typing… Dahliabitch04 is typing…

Dahliabitch04: You're not serious.

Lauren666: I am.

Dahliabitch04: You didn't come here.

Lauren666: I did.

Dahliabitch04: No, you didn't.

Lauren666: Baby, I like you a lot, and I want this to be real.

Dahliabitch04: I'm going to throw up. This is too much. We just met.

Dahliabitch04: I don't even fucking know you.

Dahliabitch04: Oh my god, I think I'm having an anxiety attack.

Lauren666: Baby, calm down. We can get a cup of coffee and relax. Let me pick you up.

Dahliabitch04: I don't know what to do.

Lauren666: What about your dream? You just said you wanted to give us a chance. Well, now you can.

Lauren666: Don't you want this to be real like I do?

Lauren666: I want to wake up next to you. I need to actually be here for that to happen.

Dahliabitch04: No. Fuck no.

Dahliabitch04: There's no way you're coming over here. I'm going to report your account.

Lauren666: What? No, don't. Just give me a chance. Please.

Lauren666: Dahlia, I drove all this way for you. I see something in you that I've never seen in anyone and...I just need to know what your eyes look like. I wanna see you in motion. You called me to see me in action but not talk to me. That was creepy! You're a creepy person too!

Lauren666: I just want to see you move and know that you're alive. I want to feel the life in you. Is that so horrible?

I'm crying now. I'm crying my makeup off my eyes because I fucked up. I did exactly what I thought I would do.

I always do this.

I always fucking do this.

Goddamn it.

Dude, I miss my dad.
Fuck. I'm sorry, Dahlia.
I just miss Dad.
I can't take it.
I should kill myself.

Dahliabitch04 is typing… Dahliabitch04 is typing…

I could do it here. Here is a beautiful place in the green, green grass.

Dahliabitch04: If my mom finds out that I had a girl come to the house, she will make my life a living hell. We can't stay here.
Lauren666: I can pick you up.
Dahliabitch04: I don't know you…
Lauren666: What would it take? What would it take for you to feel like you know me enough to leave with me?
Dahliabitch04: Leave with you? I don't know. It's only been three days.
Lauren666: But you love me.
Dahliabitch04: What? I just met you!
Lauren666: You do. I know you feel this thing I feel too. You feel dangerous to me too. You feel like playing Russian roulette. I feel like I'm ready to blow up the whole fucking world with you. Isn't that what you said you wanted?
Lauren666: You want to dance with Dahmer? I can be Dahmer.
Dahliabitch04: I'm scared.
Lauren666: What do you have to lose?
Dahliabitch04: This is crazy. I can't do this.
Lauren666: Fuck your mom. Don't you want to be independent? All by yourself? Empowered? You can be Dahlia all you want around me. I'll never ask you to be the person your parents wanted. I'll never pretend you're someone you're not. You can just be Dahlia.
Lauren666: And Lauren and Dahlia can hit the road and

never be seen again. You can find a new home where the only people that know you know you as Dahlia. The sweetest girl in the world with the picnic table dress.

Lauren666: And I could love you, Dahlia. Imagine that. Imagine my love.

Dahliabitch04: I've never been in love.

Lauren666: Me neither.

Dahliabitch04: I'm scared.

Lauren666: Me too.

8.

Lauren is parking her car down the street just out of sight, and I swear I'm going to have a heart attack. I can feel my eyes involuntarily dancing in terror.

I grab a backpack from the closet and pull it open. It's my favorite one, with a little red dinosaur on it. I've had it since I was a kid. I fill it with syringes, estradiol valerate, only three months' worth. A large bag of pills goes into the backpack.

I lift my makeup drawer off its hinges and dump it into the bag. I rush off to my bedroom. I have so many clothes, but Dahlia only has a few. Dahlia is all that matters now, so I couldn't give a shit about the rest of this place. It can all burn for all I care. I should burn it down when I run out. I'm Dahlia now.

I'm just Dahlia now.

I grab exactly three dresses from under my bed and stuff them into the bag, and then I put my ear to the ground to listen. There's a television somewhere, but I can't tell if it's in the living room or one of the bedrooms. I have to slip out without a single person noticing until at least morning. People file missing person reports all the time, and they're just never found. Maybe I got eaten by alligators. Why not?

Either way, when someone comes looking for me, they will say, "Yes, we're looking for {**REDACTED**}" and I'll say, "Oh, I'm so sorry, no one by that name lives here."

I think about this all the time. This poisonous thought worked itself into my psyche years ago and won't ever let me go. It's beyond living your truth. It's living your fiction. If we never get away from our truth, how will we ever be something bigger than ourselves? I want to be a myth, and yet here I am, living my truth.

Lauren genuinely scares me. Sometimes after talking, I'll lie awake at night and think about her and how she makes me feel like I'm going to end up like her in less than a year. She strikes me as the kind of person who has spent most of her life trying an assortment of drugs and never really getting hooked on any. But she needs all of them all the time to function. She's like a robot that wants something from me in particular.

One day, I was lying on my bed listening to The Smiths when I saw her on my Tinder feed, and I thought longingly for a moment. I'm not even the kind of person who can show my face online, let alone do much more than that. She seemed brave to me. She clearly isn't ready to grow up, but I guess neither am I for different reasons.

Talking to her became kinda therapeutic. It was nice to feel like someone wanted to speak to me, even if I wasn't attracted to her physically. She's beautiful, but like.. I struggle with some mysterious aspect of her. It's her personality.

I like her a lot, but I see her as sad. I'm sad too, but she's clearly a lot more miserable than me. And talking to her can have the adverse effect of making me even more tragic by proxy. She's clearly the kind of person who wants to be happy but can't, for some reason.

I'm thinking beyond her now. This could be the only way out for me. Even if it has to be with her, it's better than nothing.

Lauren666: I'm parked down the street. I hope it's not too long of a walk. It's dark outside.

Lauren is concerned for my safety. I know deep down that going with her will probably kill me. But I have a death wish. I have to get out of here. I didn't want to do it with her, but the prospect of my life changing now and then dealing with it later is too tempting. I figure *anywhere* is better than here.

When I was a kid, I would imagine myself as a giant puzzle. I didn't like any of the pieces, so I imagined myself without those pieces. Even feeling blank spots where those pieces used to be made me happier. I would rather be broken than fixed if fixed meant I was designated the wrong way round. I hate my regional language.

I hate Oklahoma; I have to get out of here. I go to this support group with my mom. She makes me go. It's trans women and men that are all scared to death. Some are aging, and that scares them. Some are dealing with violence and hatred from friends and family. Then there's lil ole me.

And truth be told, I'm too crazy for them, anyway. If they knew the contents of my mind, they probably wouldn't like me anymore. But for a while, they were my friends, and I watched slowly as each one took their own life or was murdered.

I hate Oklahoma.

So I don't want to be another shitty fact about Oklahoma. I want to be a shitty fact of Lauren's. I want to be a footnote on that life instead. Wouldn't that be nice? To be someone else's problem?

She probably won't take care of me, but I can learn to take care of myself.

I sneak down the stairs, and I hear the television behind a door in the master bedroom. Mom will listen to me leave if I use a door. She will hear me if I make any sound opening a window. If I open a window on the second floor, I'll probably hurt myself. I imagine Lauren being overjoyed to see me and her joy kind of scaring me.

I tried to video-chat with her right when we met, and I kept my camera off to see how she reacts when she doesn't think anyone's around. It was cute. It endeared her to me for sure. I've always found watching other people just exist is more accurate than experiencing them directly. I figured I could have a better relationship with her if we never met.

I decide that the best way out of my life is also the most painful. Sometimes life is like that.

It hurts to help yourself.

It hurts to make life tolerable.

I have to dive out of a door and drive off into the night.

I have to make a scene. That's the only way I can get what I need. Besides, why wouldn't I want to announce my exit? Why wouldn't I want my mom to know I fucking left her? I fucking left her for a cis lesbian. Fuck you, Mom.

I sneak into the garage, and I find the gas can we keep for lawn mowing. I take it upstairs and open up my bedroom closet. I dump the contents of the gas can on my clothes. No. Not Dahlia's clothes. Someone else's clothes. Fuck these clothes and fuck you. Fuck the world. I will go somewhere no one can find me.

I light my lighter and toss it on my clothes. It's begun now.

I close the closet doors on the flames, grab my bag, and rush downstairs. Once downstairs, I hear the familiar rattle of my mom stirring from her room to see what the fuck is happening, and then I'm out the door. There's screaming, more than I expected. There's a car. Headlights. Oh my God, am I outside?

I see her face, and something is different. I can't catch it fast enough before we're off, and my mother is screaming on the front lawn, and I'm gone. I'm Sally from *Texas Chain Saw Massacre*. Laughing all the way home.

About a year later, we're down the street. I turn to look at Lauren, and something uncanny happens. I see her, but also through her as if she's not there. She's a ghost of someone. That's what I am. I used to be a teenage boy, but then I was possessed by the spirit of an Edwardian woman, and I can't get free of her. My voice changed. My body changed. I changed. I look at her, and I see a change in her. She's developing into something new, but so am I.

"Hey, bitch," she says and grins.

"We have to get the fuck out of here before she calls the cops," I spit. I look through the rearview mirror.

"Oh babe, we're getting out of here," she says.

I shoot her a look. She has perfect skin, but it looks starving for light and color. She's paler than me and blonde. She has a tiny wart on her ear.

Lauren is real. She animates her body with ease and grace.

Her fingers dance across the car and reach for the radio.

Maybe we are best friends.

Perhaps this is love, after all.

I don't know the requirements of love, but I imagine running away together under any circumstances is pretty romantic.

9.

I rescued her. I saved her life. No more chat logs. No more wondering what's next. No more swiping. She's not exactly what I expected. She's more butch than I figured. She seems like she's only recently started to push her boundaries, whereas I've been doing it forever. She's a new kind of crazy and still rough around the edges.

But she's beautiful, and she's mine.

The cum and sweat between my legs only got worse, but when I saw her, aftershocks of the orgasm I had earlier crept their way up my thighs. I felt myself stimulate the problem further. I wonder what her penis tastes like. What do girls call their penis? I have a million questions, but I don't want to ask.

All I know is she's beautiful, and she's mine, and we're riding away in the sunset. Isn't that the most poetic thing in the whole world?

"Where do we go?" I belch and feel a slight regret.

"What do you mean?" She plays coy.

"Where do we go now?" I smile ear to ear and look over at her once and then twice to prove she's real. I should pull the car over and kiss her, but what I have to do is find us a place. I don't know what we need to do, but we need a place, and we need it soon. I can feel the need rising in her too. Her eyes scream a need that mine have been crying about since I was born. Fuck me. Fuck me. Save me. Fuck me.

"I thought I was staying at your place?"

"Yeah, baby, but that's three *hours* away…" I can't tell if she catches my drift.

Hotels are cheap.

No one is traveling.

There's hardly a car on the road.

We could stay anywhere we wanted, and we could be as loud as we wanted.

"Do you want to get a room?" I ask. Transparency is surprisingly necessary.

"Not here," she says. "We have to leave the state."

I'm exhausted. I'm drenched in sweat, and I haven't gotten a chance to do much more than sit in this car all day. Having this girl really helps, but I can't ignore my physical limitations. Regardless of how hard my loins throb, I need to sleep.

"I've been awake for forty-five hours, and I need to get some sleep," I say, and she agrees.

"I'm sorry," she says. "I just don't want to die in Oklahoma."

I understand. I don't want to die here, either. I feel so foolish about my suicidal ideation when I think about the green grass. Something I should have enjoyed but instead used selfishly. I should only ever want to die in the place that I want to give my body to. Taking from the land would be wrong.

"We can survive one more day here, and I promise," I say, "home will be waiting for you."

Imagine it. The light is pouring in my old, haunted house. The bleak, dreary landscape is now full of life. I love the way she animates her face. How she controls her micromotion. She can do that to the house too. Maybe then my dad will find a new place to live. Heaven or Hell: either would be fine.

Lauren smells intensely like sweat. I take my clothes off in the dark and turn on my side, so she won't be tempted to interact with me. First impressions are everything, and this one is horrible. I start to regret my decision lying here in the dark, but it's too late now.

I wonder if my mother is dead. Did she burn when she went upstairs and opened my bedroom door? Maybe the sheer force of new oxygen blew her backward on fire. I hear that if a bomb goes off in your face, the first thing you lose is your ears. I imagine my mom's ears flying off her head, going splat onto the wall behind her. I suddenly feel less regret.

Sleeping next to someone you don't trust is a harrowing experience. You lie in the dark waiting for the point of a knife or the scramble for a weapon. You prepare. Step one: Turn on my back and smash her nose into her skull. She should die instantly, but if she doesn't, I'll have to hit it a lot more times. The most significant risk is getting a bone stuck in my wrist and bleeding out. If she scrambles, I'll have to run.

I don't imagine anything is going to happen to me, though. More than anything, Lauren seems to want to help me. She looks sweet, but it's hard to tell through layers of sweat. She smells so bad that I struggle to even see her. What I do see is melted makeup and phlegm on her chin.

Being close to her is a big problem. I'm as far as I can be from her, but I still smell her, and I still fear her touch. I still expect her to hurt me. I am still preparing.

I can't tell what her angle is.

What is my life supposed to be now? Where are we going? Who am I going to be? I don't know where she lives, but I know it isn't here. I don't know who I'm going to be, but it won't be me. Anything is better than this. Anything is better than me.

So I guess I don't care what happens to me. I don't care what happens tomorrow. Even if the worst imaginable thing were to come true tomorrow, it couldn't be as bad as one more day at home. Home is gone, and I have to be my own home now. I killed my mom, and I have to become my own mother now. I burned my mom alive to be reborn in her ashes.

Mom says, "What are we going to do about Lauren?"

Mom says, "Do we need to kill her too?"

I've never killed anyone before. Other than my mom, I guess, but that was happenstance. And besides, she might not even be dead.

I could turn over, grab Lauren's neck, and force her out

cold. I could smash her nose into her brain. I don't have anything I could stab her with. Then I remember my injectable estrogen. I could use a needle. She would never see it coming if I was quick.

I could penetrate her with a needle in the right place to make it quick. I could inject air into her veins, and she would die in minutes.

My eyes migrate across the room to my bag, and I consider how loud or quiet I could get there and back. I don't even know if Lauren's sleeping, and I want her to think I'm sleeping, so I can't check.

Fuck.

I think I could kill someone. I imagine watching life leave someone's eyes and guiding them through that archway, and it's almost poetic. Killing Lauren might be giving her everything she ever wanted. Maybe she's miserable and just waiting for someone to save her from herself.

I've seen people die before. A lot, actually. I spent much of my life obsessed with watching it happen. I watched as idiot assholes killed their friends with hammers and bats. I saw a guy have his face cut off. I've watched footage of mothers holding their mutilated children. I've watched so many suicides, but the murders always bother me. The screaming bothers me. It gets to me dreadful, and some nights when I try to sleep, I can still hear all that screaming.

I know no one is in this hotel. I know I can do whatever I want, and no one will hear me. But I don't know if I can go through with it while Lauren screams. I can't imagine stabbing her over and over. It would take so many cuts. I'll have to cover her face with a pillow and strangle her. Gurgling, I can handle. If I can stop her screaming, I think I can kill her.

I need to know if she's awake, but I don't know how to find out without attacking her. If I spring on her, I can get the jump on her. If she's prepared for me, then I will probably die. But if I can get on top of her, secure her hands, cover her face and choke her, she won't be able to do much other than writhe. Then I can take her car and go wherever she lives. I can just live there, and maybe I can just be her.

I think about the name Lauren. Am I a Lauren? Am I a Dahlia? What fits me more? Which is more like me? Does it matter? This is about survival. I have to focus on what's important. If I have to be Lauren, then I can be Lauren. I'll be the best Lauren anyone ever saw. I'll need to bleach my hair, but I've always wanted to be a blonde.

She stirs around behind me. I feel the urge hit. This is beyond functionality to me. I think I want to kill her. That would probably be for the best. I think it would be doing her a favor. I think about my mom's ears flying off her head, and I think about the blessing I must have done to the world. I rid the world of her. Maybe I could rid the world of Lauren. That would be doing the world a favor too. If she gets me back, then I can't help but think that the world will also have been paid a blessing if I die. I have to kill her.

I think about Bud Dwyer, and I exhale. One. Two. Three.

All at once, I'm on her. My legs spread easily and slide directly onto her pelvis. I grab her hands, pull them over her head, and hold them tightly, searching them for any threat. I can't find one. I expect her to start screaming, but she doesn't. I look down and notice that she's asleep. She's decided to make this really easy for me.

I grab the pillow that was under my head and throw it over her calm face. I hope the dream she's having is peaceful. I run my hands up her shoulder blades and onto her neck. She will wake up immediately when I cut off her air supply. There will be no going back at that point. I relax my forearms and shoulders, and looking down at the pillow, I squeeze with all my might.

Her throat closes with no effort. I can feel the pressure build in her lower neck, and suddenly, her arms come alive and attempt to move. They struggle and struggle but can't seem to get free under my knees. I wonder if she's thinking about me under there or if she's unsure. Does it even matter?

It occurs to me that this isn't what she wants at all. I was trying to do her a favor, but she can't possibly feel comfort.

She can't see what a favor this really is if she doesn't know it's me! I release her and hear her gasp. I rip the pillow away from her face, and she's covered in tears and phlegm. I grab her neck again.

"Shh. Sh. Sh. Sh." I encourage her, but she struggles even more. Now she's looking into my face and screaming with her eyes. It's horrible. She's screaming and gurgling silently, and her fingernails dig into my knees. She goes through emotional stages, first a nightmare, but then sadness and terror, then anger.

She pushes me with her pelvis, and my legs jerk. She gets a small gasp of air before thrusting again and using the leverage to get one of her knees between us.

The knee distracts me just long enough for her arm to get free. Her left arm grabs at her throat and rips at my hands. Then all at once, like a snake shedding its skin, she pulls me from her body with her legs, and my hands are off her neck. She gasps and coughs but knows that she has to kill me first if she means to survive.

Immediately, she screams and lunges at me, and I know she has no mercy in her.

10.

I was born a pale grey worm. I writhed, and that was all. My existence was so simple—a dance. I writhed with my little family until my little worm family was gone. Then I wiggled with my friends. We wiggled all day long. But then my friends stopped twitching and started lying around, and then they wouldn't come when I wiggled near them. Soon I was the last worm left squirming. I wiggled and wiggled until wiggling hurt me. It hurt me so bad that I had to quit wiggling and lie down. I knew I would soon die a pale grey worm.

I wake up in total darkness. I can't breathe. Something landed hard on top of me in the night. It covered my eyes. It crushed my hips. It choked me, and I know soon it will kill me. My name is Lauren, and I will die a pale grey Lauren. I feel the darkness grip me, and then I think about dad again. The last face a daughter wants to see when she goes. But I can't be free of him.

One day he was here, and the next, he was gone. He didn't go anywhere. He left and was never seen again. I start to understand where he went and what that place is like. After staring at the blackness for long enough, you see vivid images. I see Dahlia right at the end.

She takes my darkness away, and then there she is, on top of me. Her beautiful brown hair covering her left eye. Her features are so small and mousey.

I watch her hands reach firmly around my neck and squeeze. It's everything I hoped for, and I let the air leave my lungs. I feel a cold chill press its way down my back. My legs loosen and fill with euphoria. My breathing becomes impossible, and I feel the blood pool in my face. My eyes lock with hers, and I see the love that I have come to know.

She's everything I could have possibly hoped for. She couldn't wait to have me.

I imagine her lying awake, wishing that I would wake up, kiss her, hold her, and stroke her hair. I imagine her hoping she could push her dick into me. I imagine her wanting to grip onto me when she felt my insides absorb her. My neck is the perfect place to hold, and I am just a tube, after all. I feel my guts churn with terror, and my soul quiver in preparation for annihilation.

She doesn't let up. She grips me until I worry that I'm going to pass out. I've been choked several times, and the black dots in my vision tell me that I'm not long for this world. She's so sweet and inexperienced. I heave my weight in the air to pull my legs to my chest. If I can get leverage, I can pry her off of me and then show her how this needs to be done. She needs someone to teach her how.

I heave myself and success! I manage to get my legs free and then my hands. Just as I see the blackness taking me, I take a massive gulp of air and flip the script. Then I'm on top of her, and I grab her wrists and hold them down by her sides. She kicks with all her might but can't get an angle to shift my weight. I sit firmly on her pelvis, and she seizes violently under me to get away.

But there's no escaping me now.

I spit on her face. Some falls into her open mouth.

"Fuck you for that, bitch." I spit again. This time in her eyes. "Fuck you."

She starts screaming. It quickly bypasses the friendly and sexual screams I'm used to and goes straight into a guttural panic scream. It makes me think of a rabbit being crushed alive.

I spit into her screaming mouth. Her disgust makes me giggle to myself. She retches and gags and spits down the side of her face. And even though I hadn't planned this, I see her look up at me and know that she is truly mine. She has never felt so helpless in her whole life. How could I not fall in love with someone so innocent? I ease my head down to her lips and kiss her. I feel her lips lock with mine, and for a moment, I know I'm in control.

She is repulsed and immediately headbutts me. I can feel a pain in my nose grow, and blood rushes down my face. I lean back and start crying. It's involuntary. If I could stop, I would, but I'm hurt. My face hurts, but the rejection kills me inside. I consider letting her hands go and letting her do all the other things she wants to do. Maybe I deserve this.

"Fuck you." She spits up at me.

But then I realize that this is a challenge. Dahlia gives me information about what she likes, and it's a little rougher than I'm used to. I look down at her and see her satisfaction with the damage she caused. I snort as much blood from my nose as possible and hold it in my mouth. The crimson taste of iron. I spit the blood on her face.

"I want to hurt you," I lean down and whisper. "I want to hurt you real bad."

And I do. She's seen me bleed, but I haven't seen her bleed. And I want to. But I've never hurt anyone as bad as she has hurt me. I consider all the possible ways to harm her back. I'm doomed if I let her go.

"Stop," she screams. "Don't!"

But I know what I have to do. I slam my face into her collarbone and bite down hard on the bone. She screams in agony and pleasure. I feel a fire brew inside my abdomen, and I know at once that this is a new turn-on. I've never done something so violent, and it makes me feel like my every sensory input is orgasmic. The control makes me feel like I can do anything.

At first, the bite is hard but gentle enough to keep the skin intact. But then I grip Dahlia's collarbone harder and harder, and her screams turn from mild to life or death terror. Then with ease, the sharpness of my teeth passes through her skin like jello.

I taste sweet blood.

I can taste her precious blood.

It's metallic bliss on my tongue.

She shakes violently, doing anything she can to detach me. But the more she moves and I don't let go, the deeper I sink and the harder she screams. My teeth grind against her collarbone.

"Lauren," she begs. "Please stop. You're hurting me."

I can hear her pleading, and her screams, but I'm fixated on her blood now. Something in her blood makes me not care. I don't care if she is hurt. I don't care if she wants me to stop. I can do anything I want to her now. She's mine. I've tasted her insides.

I let go, and I sit back up, my mouth covered in both of our blood. It pools together like a miraculous soup, and I can't help but smile. My dreams are all coming true.

"Now you do me," I say and let go of her wrists. She's more like me than I could have ever known before.

I scramble. My wrists are suddenly accessible, and I can't tell if I should use them to kill Lauren or escape. I'm not a vengeful person, but I grab Lauren by the neck and slam her against the bed. I grip her nose without hesitation, and my hand goes over her mouth, and then her hands come up to grab my wrists.

"Stop. Stop. Stop. Stop." I can feel myself getting angrier as she struggles against me. "Stop. Stop. Stop it. Stop it."

I realize that my skin is covered in cold, wet sweat, and my underwear is soaked through.

The bed is covered in blood, sweat, and phlegm.

I am covered in blood, sweat, and phlegm.

I uncover Lauren's nose to allow her a breath, and I try to regain my calm.

I think about being a kid. My dad took me to this big playground every other weekend after my parents divorced. There was a vast forest area behind the playground, and I used to get lost there for hours. One time, they even sent the police in search of me because I would just disappear. Look at me now.

Lauren digs her nails deep into my wrists, and I lurch and let her go.

"Goddammit," I spit. I stare at her. We're only three feet

apart. She could make a move on me before I even think about it. I should think about it. I could go for the needles in my bag.

"Why are you going easy on me now?" she says with spite. Her words are swallowed gum that she's coughing back up.

Why am I? Why can't I carry out my own plan? She's asking for it. She wants me to do harm, and I can't. I can't even do it when she wants me to.

"I'm confused," I admit, defeated. "And my collarbone hurts really bad."

For a second, I catch concern in her eyes. It quickly dies, and she looks like a predator again. Any minute now, she's going to finish her meal. I saw a video of a lion attack once. The poor guy that the lion mauled just lay there on the ground with no idea what to do while it stalked back and forth about his body. It took pride in its new possession, and Lauren is taking pride in me. She has me now. I've given up, and she knows I'm prey. I'm going to be eaten.

But something comes over her as she approaches me. Her hands are gentle, touching the new cuts on my face. She pushes my hair behind my ear on the left side, and I can't help but feel something new. I wonder what it would have been like to grow up with a mother that loves you. I imagine a mother that takes care of me when I get hurt. I spent so much of my life hurt, and all I ever wanted was someone to clean me.

She speaks gently in my ear.

"It's okay now," she says. "Let me take care of you."

I don't want to at first. I remember the demon's gaze atop my chest, spitting blood on my defenseless face. Surely care and kindness couldn't come from the same person. I resign myself to the knowledge that this is a trick. At any moment, Lauren will finally do me in. She'll lure me into comfort, and she'll take her opportunity to protect herself, and she'll kill me. If I were her, I would do that to me.

But as her hands calm me, I can't help but relax and feel the new sensation. Her touch is non-judgemental. I forget that I was born in a body that disagreed with me. In the past, whenever a partner would make an attempt to touch me, I would recoil in terror. The idea of someone knowing all of me is something I fear deeply.

My secrets protect me.

"Dahlia," she says. "How are you so perfect? Did you fall from the sky?"

I can't believe what I'm hearing. I don't understand. Who could possibly understand? My fears of danger wash away into pure confusion. We spent the last hour trying to kill each other, and now she thinks this is a healthy thing.

"What are you doing to me?" I shout. "Get the fuck off me!"

I push her but not hard enough to cause any damage. She takes the rejection hard. I feel bad for a moment, but I can't possibly understand.

"I'm just trying to love on you. I don't want to fight you anymore." There's a weakness in her voice now. She's grown hoarse over the day, and at this point, there's hardly anything left.

"But I hurt you," I say, trying to reason with her.

"I hurt you too," she says. "And I liked it."

I liked it. I think about this phrase and its connotations. The possibility is that if I stay with Lauren, I will be getting hurt on the regular. She wants me to be her voodoo doll.

"That scares me," I say. "I don't think I like that."

She turns, her face contorted and twisted into confusion. Her whole body turns. Soon her hands are on me again. Soon she's directly in front of me.

"I can teach you how to like it."

PART II: PLAY

11.

Did you know you get unlimited free drinks at just about any casino in Oklahoma? Weed is legal here, too, for the medically inclined. But for our purposes, it's all about the free drinks. I walk around the vast building of lights and sounds. We're in an adult arcade filled with smoke and old white people that genuinely think tonight could be the most excellent night of their life. Everyone is here to score and hit it big. I guess I am too.

She's so perfect that I can barely contain myself. My neck hurts from her grasp, but nothing has ever made me hornier. It was everything I'd hoped for, and I didn't even have to have the awkward, "Please, choke me" conversation. My teeth ache from gripping her collarbone so hard. Electricity shoots through my veins when I remember grinding my teeth on her bones.

I can't imagine how she feels. She keeps a solid poker face. She wears this sleek black dress that's velvet, and her hair is recently brushed and washed. But I know she's like me now. I know we're the same, and thus I can take her right where I know she wants to go.

In the middle of the casino floor, between a million slot machines and even more pathetic gamblers, is a kiosk that will give you all the coffee you can drink. I'm drinking all the coffee they will allow. The casinos never close, and you can easily bum coffee and cigarettes until an opportunity arises.

Being a woman in a casino with a lovely dress and hair and nails and face will get you into many bizarre circumstances. It's easy to make money in a place like this, but it's also easy to die. Everything here is a risk, but Dahlia doesn't know that.

I see a new light in her as if something was removed. Now the happiness flows out everywhere. The lights and sounds rattle around and dance between her eyes.

It's easy to have a death wish when there's a disease that threatens to kill you. I can't help but imagine Dahlia dying of Covid like Dad.

But tonight is a date, and we need to look our best. If we get sick, it's part of our risk.

It's so easy to be her. She walks around, and everyone stops and looks. She parts a crowd without any effort, and now I understand why she doesn't leave the house. Everyone is looking.

Soon, everyone *is* looking, and their faces warp in my mind to something else. I see a terror in her start to grow, and it's not long until we're looking for somewhere with fewer people. The casual glances become bullets, and I don't know how to intervene and protect her. I don't know what it would take to save her from all the attention, but we finally find a place to relax. She has visible sweat pooling on her forehead and upper lip. I reach out to wipe it away with the tail of my shirt, but she flinches when I touch her.

For a moment, I'm hurt again.

I'm hurt that Dahlia still doesn't trust me even when I've shown her all the care, love, and acceptance in the world. She's never had a friend like me before, and she treats me like I'm hurting her. A tear slips out the side of my eye, and I try to catch myself before any others try to sneak their way out.

"*Honey*, it's just sweat," I beg.

"We should get a drink." She takes off walking without a moment's thought.

The bar is quiet and lonely. The bartender is a short-haired blonde dyke. She's the kind of girl I would go for if I wasn't taken. Usually, this would drive me wild, but Dahlia makes everything else so quiet. I get a flutter in my gut, and I think about her hands around my neck.

"I need a double rum and Coke," she says and produces five dollars. Then after a moment, the drink materializes. Then just a moment later and the alcohol is gone.

Dahlia has had a long day. She moved out of her house, and she lives with me now! That's a lot in one day. If anyone has earned a drink, it's her. If anything, she's earned more than just a drink. It wouldn't be hard to find drugs here. An idea forms in my head, and at first, I consider that it might be too evil. But I know she likes me because I'm a little evil, so maybe she'll like it more than she could understand. I start scanning the small crowd around the slot machines, interested in pushing little-miss-inexperienced out into the world. Maybe I can make someone luckier than they could ever imagine.

All at once, I catch him behind a slot machine with a cigarette in one corner of his mouth. He's in his mid to late forties, and he's too cool to be a dad. He's got that edge of someone who wants to live their fantasy tonight. Some people come here to win, but luck can come in a billion different shapes. He's living in a fantasy world, and we are just two cartoon characters like him. He will pay for anything we want all night. We can get all the drugs we wish. Dahlia deserves to get fucked by a man like that. Dahlia deserves to experience the power and anger and angst, and this man has that.

"Do you like drugs?" I blurt out while squinting in Mr. Right's direction.

"I've never done anything harder than weed and booze," she says.

I feel bad for her.

I could help her.

I could save her from sobriety.

She could fix her disposition so quickly.

Guys like that usually have cocaine, but I want MDMA. I want to get her in a hotel room with MDMA and sex. She needs this.

"Come with me," I say and begin my approach. As if I'm pouncing on a lion, I creep up to him and stand at his shoulder. Dahlia catches up slowly, leading with her legs as if drunk but nervous.

"Excuse me!" I shout at him. "My friend just ran by here. We're looking for her."

He turns to look at us. His gaze is like a towel soaking up

water. He pulls the cigarette out of his mouth, and it makes me shiver. This is precisely the man we need.

"What?" he shouts.

"My friend!" I shout back. "We're looking for her. Have you seen *Molly*?"

This trick always worked when I was in high school, searching for drugs among strangers. A cute girl walks up and asks for drugs, and she may as well be sucking you off. She's opening her mouth for you, and every guy has an oral fixation.

The idea of doing drugs with Dahlia makes me feel an elation I haven't felt since I was a child. I feel like I have a new best friend, and we get to do best friend shit now!

"No, I haven't seen anyone." He turns back around, clearly understanding my game. I sit at the slot next to him. It starts like this, but he knows that I'm not asking for drugs. I have to show him I'm persistent if I want the night he promises.

"Hi," I say. "I'm Sarah, and this is my sister, Deborah. But you can call her Debbie."

He looks at me, then at Debbie.

"It's a pleasure," he says to Debbie, then to me.

"The pleasure is all ours," I say and smile. I wonder if Dahlia still thinks we're looking for drugs.

"Well," I say. "If you didn't see our friend Molly running around, then maybe you've seen some of the *rest* of our group running around. Can you help me find *someone*?"

I love to play pathetic.

"I'm *lost*," I say, then make a frowny face.

"Look, my wife is here with me, and I can't do this," he mutters. "If you meet me at the bar at two in the morning, after she's asleep, I might be able to help you both. But you need to get lost right now."

"Yessir!" I say and stand up. "It's been a pleasure, sir."

Then I grab Debbie's hand, and we walk back to the bar. She is confused but game, nevertheless. If we hide in the bar and get Debbie one more drink, it should calm her nerves enough to really party. This will be the most excellent night

68

of her life.

"Happy birthday, little girl," I smile.

It's the first day of Debbie's new life, and I created her. She's made in my image. This means I get to feed her all the details.

"What are we trying to do?" she pries.

"I'm trying to show you a good time for once," I say. "Listen, you need to loosen up a bit. Guys don't like it when you don't act confident. I know that you have a lot going on, but if you want to have *fun* tonight, you need to get another drink and try to relax."

"We're not spending the night with *him*, are we?" she asks.

"We're going to have a drink with him and see if we can score anything," I say. "There's more to this than just drugs. We could get a lot out of him, which might help us get where we need to go. We need petty cash, and guys like that are loaded with it. He probably brought money for a prostitute and stuffed it in his shoe just in case he got the chance. This is his lucky day, and we get to *take* that money. We can take his drugs and his money, and we can run."

It's a good case. I would do it.

"He's going to get really pissed off if we take his money and run," she says. "What if he attacks us?"

I hadn't considered the tangible dangers. I think about ways we could protect each other, and they're myriad. I'm not worried at all.

"If he gives us problems," I whisper, "we can just solve them."

The bartender takes a turn down the bar and walks past our seats. I raise my hand and order us each a Vodka Red Bull. I sip mine when they arrive, but Dahlia takes a whole mouthful. Immediately, she's hit with the buzz and the energy. Her eyes widen slightly, and it scares me because I can see the abyss in them. The same abyss that I know in myself. I can see myself in her. At that moment, I realize I'm not a person but a shapeless black mass floating around somewhere in a body, and so is she. When I see her, I really see her. Deep down, we're the same shapeless nothing.

69

"Let's do it," she says. "Fuck it. I've lived my whole life so scared of everything. I'm leaving that behind too. I'm so tired of being this timid person all the time. I wish I was more like you."

"Why would you ever want to be more like me?" I ask.

"You can just get up and talk to people and do things, and I'm so scared," she mutters, and trails off. She comes back with force and says, "I'm done with that. It's time for me to take control of my life. Let's do it. Let's milk this guy for whatever we can get."

"That's my girl," I say.

I'm so proud of her.

12.

It's two in the morning, and we're still sitting at the bar. There are games everywhere, but we have no interest in playing those. We have a bigger, deeper game to play. I check the time, and I know any second, our man will be leaving his hotel and entering our lives. His fate is yet to be determined, but whatever happens, I know Dahlia and I will have fun.

Debbie and Sarah laugh.

Debbie and Sarah fix each other's hair and makeup.

Debbie and Sarah are sisters.

They sit at the bar and giggle like they've known each other forever. So when the elevator doors open and he walks out and sees the sisters so close to each other, he can't help but imagine the things he wants to do to them. He's nearly fifty, and he's never been with two girls at the same time before. That's one of those mythical male conquests from a bygone time. He could cross something off his bucket list today.

He approaches, first with caution and then with fake cheesy confidence, as if we are already an open and shut deal.

"I must admit," he says to Debbie. "I didn't think you two would wait this long."

He doesn't think he deserves this. He thinks it's too good to be true for lil ole him. And he's right. This is too good for him, and that's why we're going to skin him alive and take him for everything he has. Tonight, *we* are the House, and if we put out enough gentle feelers, he will give us everything.

"So, were you able to find any of our friends?" Sarah asks. I love being the center of attention, and I love performing. Tonight, I get to share my stage, but I can show off all of my best skills. Dahlia will be so impressed.

"We should talk about your friends somewhere else," he says and gives a paranoid glance around. He smells like cheap cologne, and it makes me feel like he's going to offer us meth or Adderall.

Adderall promises a fun and long night, but it won't make us high. Meth isn't ideal for short-term adventures. We need something more straightforward than that, but harder than Addies. Men are always too much or not enough.

Going to a hotel room now would be too easy, but we can't possibly do anything here. I don't trust him, even if he's likeably stupid. It's dangerous to think someone is stupid because they could be evil in disguise. We both have our secret guns pointed at each other under the table.

"Where?" Debbie asks and reaches for his leg. I see her lurch and try to keep her composure, but the performance is difficult for her.

"Well," he turns towards her and squints. "Anywhere you want in the whole world."

And then this bitch sees the challenge and doubles down on it. I shit you not.

"I wanna go to Disneyland," she says between wet lips. He visibly shivers, and the blood in his body scurries.

"I can get us a room for a couple hours," he says. "How would that sound, ladies?"

I look to Dahlia for answers. I've been in many dangerous hotel room situations and know I can handle myself there, but she is in over her head. She is worried I won't protect her like I promised to.

"Did you know?" I say. "Today is Deborah-Jean's birthday."

There's a palpable silence while Dahlia considers whether to answer him or take ownership of her fake birthday.

"Oh?" He looks between us. "And how old is Deborah-Jean today?"

She looks like roadkill as it's being squashed by a truck. *Poor* baby.

"Don't you know it's rude to ask a woman her age?" I tell

him, and he straightens up. The pathetic dude looks between us like he blew it.

"But" I whisper and lean into his ear. "She's eighteen today. I brought her in with a fake ID."

The truth is, I didn't need to have an ID at all. Dahlia wasn't carded at the door, and neither was I. It's funny. In places like this, everyone just assumes you're the legal age, but they're all secretly hoping you're younger.

I look down at his denim lap and catch his erection, getting challenging to hide.

"Well, we should get a drink for the birthday girl then," he announces. "Shouldn't we?"

His smile is the gross smile of someone who hasn't taken a break from smoking in ten years. Today is the most important day of his life because when you're a fifty-year-old guy, you can't see a girl's age. We're all eighteen to him if we try hard enough.

He hollers for the bartender, throws a twenty-dollar bill on the bar, and says, "Three vodka cranberries." A spicy choice for a spicy evening. By this point, Dahlia has had a lot to drink, affecting her ability to control herself. I can see the persona she's developed. It takes over and then lets her go before taking over again.

We drink the vodka cranberries, and it does precisely what he intends for it to do. After a few minutes, Dahlia is touching him, and so am I. Soon, he looks like the pressure will make him explode. He will do anything to have us for just a minute. Even if only to tell his friends about the big fish he caught one night in the middle of a casino in the southwestern United States.

"So." He puts his glass down and looks between the two of us like we're the cutest animal he's ever seen. "Should I get us a room for a couple hours?"

Dahlia looks ready to make the leap now. The drinks have made her hopeless for an exit strategy, however. It's going to be impossible to pull him off her when the time comes to grab his shit and go.

"Hold on," I sober up. "Let's talk about money. How

much?"

A wave of anguish rolls over his face when he realizes that we didn't just *like* him. He thought that his personality took him this far. He thought two girls were attracted to him. But then he resigns himself to what he already knew deep down.

"I have a hundred dollars," he says with shame.

Dahlia sits up and lets him go. She stares at me with confusion as if I've failed her.

"No, girls," he pleads. "I have drugs. I have more money, but I would have to go back to my room to get it. If we can just get to a room, I can talk more about this."

"Alright, Debbie-Jean," I announce. "I'll bet Momma's getting worried sick, so we oughta get you home."

"Oh yes, big sister," she says. "I'm getting *really* tired now."

He looks like a blister that's about to pop.

"Girls, please!" he shouts.

I wait patiently for a good reason, but one doesn't present itself. He inches closer to me and says, "I need this. I need her. I want her."

"Well," I whisper back. "She's expensive. She's rare."

He leans back quickly and finishes his drink. "I'm gonna run over to that ATM right now, and what do you say I pull out $500, and then we go get a really nice room? We can order drinks to the room, and I can show you all the goodies I found. And maybe if we have a lot of fun, we can talk about where that $500 can go. Does that sound more fair, ladies?"

And yes, it does.

It takes seconds after he leaves for Dahlia to grab me and scream under her breath. She pants and pants then exhales and straightens back up.

"What do we do if he tries to hurt us?" she asks quietly.

"If he touches you, I will cut his head off," I smile.

"If we do drugs with him, won't that impair our ability to defend ourselves?" she asks.

"The drugs are for us," I say. "We won't get that far,

74

sweetheart. We'll be out of here in an hour."

"Okay," she says. "I really love myself right now."

And I love her too. This is the version of her that I always felt in there. I knew she would be my best friend. I knew she would be the perfect addition to my little life. She's the ideal partner in crime, and I love her. I need to tell her. I need to tell her before he gets back.

"This is for us," I say. "Ya know?"

"What do you mean?"

"You can do whatever you want with him," I say. "He's my gift to you. We can share him, or we can use him to have each other. But he's yours to do whatever you want. And no matter what happens, I'll always catch you when you fall."

She stares at me and reads my face. Her eyes widen, and her abyss comes out to meet mine. Her nothingness meets mine in the middle, and I catch her darkness and show her the love that she's never known.

"I trust you," she says.

"Alright, ladies," he says, walking back up to us. "If you're ready to go there, I'm ready to take you."

I turn to Dahlia and smile with love. "Lead the way, sweetheart."

13.

I lift my legs, and the air catches me. I float above the ground like an angel. I flow through the room, and everyone watches. My grand exit into the spiritual dimension of magic and witchcraft. I dance myself out the door.

I'm flying, Mom.

He holds me still, and she keeps me still, and I can feel myself lift into the sky, held down only by my wrists. I'm a tiny red balloon, and I could fly. I'll go everywhere and anywhere, and if I get too high, I'll just pop.

The elevator makes me fly even higher, and then we're high in the sky. I look out the window, and I imagine flying like a bird right out of here. Lauren and I are flying to Paris or Rome or Kenya, or Kyoto and imagining our life there. I'm window-shopping for a new life in the sky, and I see the flatlands so grey. I wish I could paint the hills.

Sarah ushers me into my new home, and I'm immediately impressed by human ingenuity. It's the most enormous room I've ever been in, and I know what it's like to be beautiful and live beautifully. Rich, white people live like this. If my womanhood is my ticket to this, then I think I can live. I've never wanted to be rich, but there's something so beautiful about extravagance to me. I want all the expensive perfumes. I want all the expensive dresses and makeup.

Sarah pulls me to the bed, and suddenly he's next to me, and I hear Sarah say, "What do you have for us?"

He pulls a little baggy out of the back of his pants.

The contents are a variety of things that I don't understand.

He has a couple bumps of cocaine and three Adderall.

He immediately suggests we all take the Adderall so we can stay up all night, but Sarah intervenes.

"I got a guy up in Oregon who works for the cartel," he smiles.

"Our baby Debbie has a little heart condition, so I worry about giving her anything that would wake her up too much," she says. But I'm not afraid of cocaine. I would snort it. I'm not scared of Adderall; I can just stay up all night long. I consider ditching the plan and taking whatever drugs this man will give me.

I reach my hand out, snatch the baggy of drugs from his hand, and look in it with intent. I pour the pills out, and I hold them in my hand, and just like that, I find myself floating over the bed again. I take a tiny speck of cocaine and snort it up my nose.

Everyone is staring at me, confused, as if I was doing something wrong, but I can't figure out what I'm doing wrong. Sarah grabs my hands, and then I fall backward on the bed and start laughing. Then I can't stop laughing. I laugh so hard that I begin to pee myself a little. I get up and rush myself to the bathroom.

I sit down to pee, and it relieves much of my anxiety, but then I feel dizzy, and I lie on the bathroom floor. Sarah comes rushing in. She lifts me up, and I'm overjoyed to see her. She's wonderful tonight. She asks me if I'm okay, and I tell her I am. I just had too much to drink. Then he's there too, and he's looking down at us with admiration.

We're *such* a pretty sight. Sarah is cute.

He gets down on the tile floor and inches his way over to me. He reaches a hand out and quickly snatches one of my feet. I feel something grip my insides, and I lean my head back. My head lands in Sarah's lap, and I look up and see her smiling.

He kisses my foot from toe to heel and back. I start to feel a jetting explosion crash up my legs, and I can't help but giggle and squirm. Sarah pets my hair and sweetly kisses me on the head. Her left hand moves across my injured collarbone, and I wince. I cry out a bit, and she quickly covers my mouth.

His hands rush up my legs and grip my thighs under my dress. I squeeze my legs together and wince. Sarah pushes her hands down my shoulder to my breast. She gently caresses below me and then eases her way up.

I feel like I'm being taken apart and devoured by two wolves, but I'm so happy to be eaten.

I feel my dick get hard, and terror and panic pour over me. I realize that neither of them have seen my dick, and he doesn't even know I have one. Did he even know I was trans? Was I so drunk that my body just slipped my mind? How will he react?

I clench my whole body in preparation for pain. I squeeze my eyes closed. Sarah squeezes my breast, but I feel nothing but pain. Then all at once, it happens. His hand reaches between my legs and rubs around. I gasp and cry. He finds my dick, and then he grips it. I bite my lip.

He gently caresses me, and I cry out in terror and pleasure. Sarah covers my mouth harder and runs her hand down my dress and pulls it up. I'm naked in front of two people that aren't like me at all. They don't know what it's like to feel so wrong. They don't know what it's like to feel that violation by God.

I close my eyes and look for something to comfort me, but only find darkness.

I try to think of a memory that could protect me and justify me.

I wish I had a memory that made this make sense in my life.

I wish I could point to an experience in my life and say that this is why this is happening to me. But there's nothing.

It's only me.

I'm more scared than I've ever been in my life, and then I feel his wet mouth reach the tip of my dick, and I squirm to avoid it. But Sarah holds me down, and his mouth grips my dick and pulls. My eyes shoot open, and I see her staring down at me.

I beg her for salvation.

I beg her with my eyes and my screams, but she just looks down. She just enjoys my torment.

I grab his head and shove my dick down his throat. He gags and coughs and spits out my dick. Sarah lets me go, and I stumble to a standing position. My dress falls back down my naked body. I look between the two of them, and my eyes start to focus. He's coughing and gagging, and she's looking up at me with anticipation.

The whole room is spinning, and I know that I'm in no position to defend myself.

She's waiting for my direction.

"Fucking grab him," I scream at Lauren. She springs into action and tackles him. I shake my head to see clearly and step towards them. He struggles and struggles but doesn't understand the situation. I crawl over to him, sit on his lap, grab him by the sides of his head, and press it against the wall.

Terror fills his face, and his hands give up. I ease my body down on him and feel his cock is raging under his jeans. The discomfort must be significant.

Then all at once, he starts laughing.

"Y'all are fucking amazing," he laughs.

Sarah and Debbie laugh too.

Everyone laughs.

I feel something inside me burst out, and then I'm possessed by a new demon. She isn't the ghost of an Edwardian woman, no. She wants to cause hell. I reach an epiphany.

Everyone who has ever killed anyone has had to do what I'm doing now. Every one of those people had to look their victim in the eye and play a role. Every one of them felt terrible about what they had to do, but they did it anyway. They pushed through their empathy and their instincts. They were brave enough to do the thing that scared them the most.

"Alright," I hear myself say. "We're going to rob you. Whatever you have, we're going to take from you, and if that goes really well, you might get to go back to the other hotel room with your wife and sleep this off so you can admit it in the morning.

"Until you deliver, we're going to torture you. We've tortured people before, and we're not afraid of what anyone might hear this high up. If you're a good boy, then I'm going to fuck you. Sarah will hold you down, and I will fuck you to please myself. After that, if you give us what we want, we will leave."

"Hey, what?!" he screams. "What the fuck?"

"It's true," Lauren says. "I'm sorry, bud."

"But if you're bad," I feel the demon in me speak with my mouth, "I will kill you with my bare hands."

At this point, he screams in protest. It takes some effort to hold him down now.

"Then," I shout. "Then I will kill your wife. I promise this is true. I burned my mother alive, and I liked it."

Lauren gasps and turns towards me quickly.

"What?" she shouts. "You did?"

I turn back to face our captive.

"Yes, I did," I laugh. "I poured gasoline on my mother, and then I lit her on fire before running out of my house. I'm wanted all over the state."

Suddenly, everything goes wrong at once. In reaction to the realization that we are going to kill him, his stomach heaves, and he vomits all over my dress. This causes the alcohol inside me to come back up, and I puke on his chest. Lauren lets go of his hands and grasps at her face to hold back her gagging. His arms scramble to get away, and I realize there's only one thing to do.

I grab either side of his head, and I bash it into the wall we're propped upon. He screams in terror. He forms full fists and punches me in my legs and my sides. I ram his head into the wall again, and he calls and spews. This time, blood comes from his nose and mouth. He punches me so hard that the air goes out of me, and then I fall down.

I crash into the tile floor hard and heave some more. Lauren rushes him and gets one more bash in before he punches her so hard in the face that she falls backward. He stands but can barely move from the dizziness and collapses to his knees.

I try to shake off the sick and look at him, but I struggle. Lauren is screaming, and blood is pouring out of her nose. I feel a raw, rough hand grab my ankle and yank. I skid across the tile floor, and then I see his face crawling up my body. I try to move out of his trajectory, and then he's got my arms. I try to maintain consciousness, but I see specks forming in my vision and feel a cloud.

He rips my dress and pulls it up my body. I can move my head, all at once. Everything is moving at twice the average speed. I watch in fast forward as he tears my legs open, no matter how hard I resist. Then he pulls his jeans down, and his cock finally is set free from the denim prison. He's utterly flaccid from the violence, but something primal in him wants to fuck me before killing me. He shares a similar demon with me at this moment. We're the same.

I know Lauren will launch upwards and rush over to me and save me any second. She's going to hit him in the head with something, and then that'll be it. She will hit him in the head one last time, and that'll be enough to take him down. I know she's going to save me.

I feel myself fade from consciousness. Whatever control I had is lost. Any second now, Lauren will save me.

He spits on his dick and pushes it against my asshole, and I try to call out to Lauren. I try to say, "Lauren, wake up." I beg Lauren to wake up and save me now. It's time. This was the plan. He jerks his dick with spit and he gasps in pleasure.

She promised she wouldn't let me get hurt.

His dick pushes into my ass an inch and then two. I find the remaining energy in myself, and I scream out. But I know no one will hear me here. No one is ever going to listen to me again. The last thing I see is Lauren. She lies there unmoving, and for the first time, I ask the worst question I can imagine.

Is Lauren dead?

Lauren is dead.

No one is coming.

He pushes in three and four inches, and I feel his screaming exhale hit my face. His breath is wet and sour and it covers my body.

No one is coming to save me.

I am alone.

I am a ball of flesh at the end of three demons playing tug-of-war. I am the rope. I am pulled and torn and then bisected. Then all at once, my flesh is dying.

My flesh is dying.

I know Lauren is going to save me.

And then I fall asleep and have a wonderful dream.

14.

The planet was blue and green when I was born. It had millions, no, billions of people living on it.

They were amazing.

They spoke many different languages.

They wrote down their ideas.

They found and lost and found and lost God in an endless cycle. They knew each other as friends, and they invented love. Love was a pure concept devoid of any pain. Love was the freedom of never having to be afraid of someone. It was an unconditional surrender to your design. It was allowing yourself to be yourself. The planet was filled with beautiful animals that called humans friends, and that relationship was an infinite ying-yang of carbon delivery and re-delivery. The cycle continued forever, and it felt lovely to be a part of such a beautiful world regardless of the conditions of my birth. I was born, and that was a miracle. It was a miracle that anything could exist at all. I was shown that gift and privilege. I was alive.

My eyes shoot open, and I see an ornate tile ceiling. My nose is filled with an ivory-tasting liquid. Blood. I think that's blood. I sit up and am unbearably dizzy. I once again flop to the ground and stare at the ceiling. So much went into every single tiny piece of tile that found its way to that ceiling. Only a human artist could create such a beautiful mosaic. It's a wonderful place to die for sure.

I sit up, and consciousness very nearly leaves me.

My eyes focus on the room, and it's a bloody mess. It's hard to make sense of what I see. I see a pile of skin lying on the cold ground, and on top of that pale skin is a violently red creature furiously pumping its body into the flesh.

I squint my eyes as hard as possible, but I still can't identify the situation. I know I need to try standing up.

The red creature smells like sickness and blood, and it screams in euphoria. I push my hands onto the bloody, wet ground and get enough of a grip to bend my knees. Then I'm standing up, and the room is spinning. The Red Devil is turning and screaming and cramming its violence into the abandoned flesh. I blink once, twice, thrice, and then I can see briefly. The red creature is covered in blood. A man. The red animal is just a man wrapped in blood.

I take one, then two, then three steps and go down on my knees behind the Red Devil. The blood smell overcomes me and makes me sick. I gag and gag, but the Red Devil howls so loud that it can't hear me. Finally, vomit comes up and complicates the dirty floor. I try to compose myself and get my senses about me.

I need to be awake.

I need to be alive.

I need to be awake.

I need to be alive.

I need to be awake.

All at once, I pounce on the Red Devil's back. A bloody rage builds inside me. I bite down on its shoulder with all my might. My teeth sink into its body like I'm biting into a cake. I grip my jaw so hard it feels like it might break off, and I hear audible clicking in my ears. The Devil removes itself from the flesh bundle and turns to face its challenger.

I remove my mouth. Flesh catches between my teeth.

I dunk instinctively as a fist pushes the wind towards me. In one motion, I grab the fist out of the air and open the hand. Then I grab a finger in each of my hands. I look directly into the Devil's black eyes.

I pull as hard as I can, and the Devil screams as its hand splits in two down the middle. The flesh parts like torn paper. As I pull it more gently, it spreads like a pair of legs. I pull as hard as I can until I feel meat tear away at the wrist. Before loosening my grip, I throw my remaining energy into the pull, and in a snap, the arm splits flesh from the bone.

The Devil screams and screams and screams, and I jump on top of him, and I look in his face, and I say, "I'm the Devil now."

Then I push my thumbs deep into his eyes. They squirt into pieces around my fingernails. And that changes his tone completely. He goes from screaming and crying to pure clarity and resolve. His humanity comes out when I remove my thumbs. He falls backward and tries with all his might to let out another scream, but he's too hoarse. He knows that he's reached the end now, and there's nothing I can do for him.

"Kill me," he begs between tears and intense panting.

And then I feel the Devil in me give me control back. I feel myself again. My name is Lauren, and I'm the biggest sweetheart you've ever met in your whole life.

Everyone loves me.

I have someone over every other night.

I have a girlfriend.

Her name is Dahlia, and she's the most beautiful woman God ever created.

All at once, the realization hits me that the pile of flesh was Dahlia. The Devil was raping Dahlia, wasn't he? I turn towards the meat and find her lifeless body lying peacefully on the cold ground where he left her.

She's hurt really bad now. And it's my fault.

I fucked up. I failed her.

Oh my God, why did I let him go?

My fucking stomach is so weak.

I'm so soft!

I let her die.

I let him rape her.

Oh my God, I let him rape her.

I pounce on Dahlia, and I shake her dead meat.

"Baby," I scream. "Please come back, honey. I'm so sorry. Don't go. Please don't go. I need you now. You have to come back."

I shake and shake and shake and shake and shake, but nothing changes. Nothing moves. I don't know if she's breathing. I check for a pulse, but I can't find one. Her skin is cold but not wooden yet.

I lean down and kiss her open mouth, and I cry, and I cry, and I scream, and I cry, but it can't change what's happened.

It can't stop this.

It can't bring her back.

I can't bring you back.

"Just kill me," the Devil spits. "Please."

I turn my focus to the Devil, and I cry. My lower lip works its way up my face into a scowl and then contorts into horror.

"No," I whisper.

I slap at Dahlia's face, and I beg God to let her go. I can't stop until something happens. I can't stop until I see her move. I have to see her eyes roll. I have to see her eyes move.

But they don't. If Dahlia's alive, she's out cold. If she's dead, then that's it. I have nothing left to live for.

I stand and fall to the sink. The blood caking my hands makes it difficult to catch a grip, but I do, and I pull myself up.

I look into the mirror, and I see a ghastly sight.

My face is bloody and beaten.

My nose is wholly caked with blood. I'm a Devil too.

I look through the mirror at the bloody mess of living death lying on the floor, and I can't help but cry. I fucked up her birthday.

15.

I find a glass, and I fill it with water. I fill my mouth with water, and it hurts. I spit it out and see blood. I drink more water, and my throat hurts. I drink more water, and my stomach hurts.

I fill the glass with more water, and I rush to Dahlia's side. I try to pour the water into her open mouth but can't get an angle. I take some water into my mouth and quickly release it into her mouth. The water just sits in the back of her throat, so I lift her head, and I hear a gurgling sound. She's surprisingly light.

I fill my mouth with more water and spit it into her mouth, and then it drains down. I hear the sound, and I think for a second she might have just passed out from the booze. I feel tremendous relief and lay her back down on the cold ground. I take a moment to look at her body, and it's worse than I thought it could be. Her ass is a bloody mess, and her genitals are caked with blood, cum, and vomit. She has bruises forming red and purple on her neck and shoulders. How long was he using her?

I turn to see if the Devil is still with us, and he is. He's lying there against the wall, slowly bleeding out like a worthless sack of shit. I decide to let Dahlia kill him when she wakes up.

I hope she wakes up.

His contorted, horrified face is desperately trying to use the eyes he no longer has. Pathetic.

I stand and run to the bedroom, where I find his wallet. There's a hundred-dollar bill in it.

He's a fucking liar too; he deserves this. I gather his credit cards and check the time. It's five-thirty AM, and I know they'll be searching for him soon. It won't be hard to find him. I have to get Dahlia to wake up, and we have to leave immediately. Both of our faces are so fucked up that no one could possibly think we were okay. We'll have to be quick.

I need to get fuck-ass's pin number before he croaks. I find a room key with a number on it, and I know this is where his family is.

I grab the baggie of drugs, instinctively do a bump of coke, and shove it in my bag on the bedside table.

I gather everything I can and shake off the stress, exhaustion, delusions, and pain.

It's been a long night. I need my girlfriend to be alive.

I need my girlfriend to be alive. I return to her side, and I see that a puddle of water has formed on the floor where her mouth is. I don't know if she swallowed the water or not. I look over at the Devil, who looks far less devilish now.

"What's your pin number?" I shout. "For your bank!"

He breathes in and out hard. His breath is escalating to an apex place where I know he will release himself. He's at the end now.

Fuck.

I rush to his side and grab his face and shake it.

"Hey fucker!" I shout. "I know you're still with me in there. What's your fucking pin number?"

He's still just breathing hard and praying under his breath.

"All right," I announce. I reach down and grab his flaccid cock. It's covered in a mixture of cum, blood, shit, and sweat. It's the pathetic dick of the kind of guy that dies on a hotel room floor. "I'm gonna destroy this if you don't tell me the fucking pin number."

He continues to breathe hard.

"When I hurt you like this, you'll wake right up," I say. "And you'll wish you were dead."

He tries to mutter. I lean closer, and yet again, I hear mutters between gurgles. I rip at his cock and pull it towards me. A noise builds in him that springs him back from the brink of death. He moans and tries to mutter and plead

88

between hard exhales. His breath is getting faster and faster and faster.

"I don't want to kill you," I say. "I want my girlfriend that you raped to kill you. But I can take your fucking dick for what you did. Now you tell me that fucking pin number, or your wife's gonna find you dickless, you fucking faggot."

I rip at his cock again, and skin comes loose like a glove coming off a finger.

He manages to hum, "Two," and then, "Four."

"Come on, you little fucker!" I shout. "Two digits. Two digits, and I won't stuff it in your mouth."

I pull, and the finger slips from the glove, and he forms a "Three" with his mouth.

"Three?" I ask. He tries to nod.

Then, with the last of his energy, he lifts his remaining hand and forms "One" with it.

"Is the last digit 'one'?" I ask with glee. He nods, and I say thank you. I release his dick, and the glove settles back on the finger.

Two, four, three, one. Two, four, three, one. Two, four, three, one. I grab Dahlia and lift her up.

"Come on, baby," I plead. "We've gotta go. You need to wake up for me, baby girl."

But she still doesn't move. I shake her so hard, and she doesn't move. I shake her so hard, and I cry so hard, and she doesn't move. I beg God, and yet she doesn't move. She won't be able to kiss me ever again. We never made love. We never talked about starting a family. I never learned about her past, and she never knew about me.

My girlfriend is dead, and I just started to love her.

I calmly stand up and walk over to the Red Devil. He exhales hard and accepts the end that's coming.

"Do you believe in God?" I ask.

He tries to nod with his last motions but fails and his head just quakes.

"Let's see if he saves you," I say and leave the room.

I'm walking.

I'm opening the door to the hotel.

I'm in the elevator.

I'm going down.

I'm walking out of the lobby.

I hide my face.

I get in the car.

I look over, and she's not in the passenger seat anymore. Instinctively, I start sobbing and look up to where I imagine the room is.

Any moment now, authorities will burst into the room, and they'll find Dahlia and the Devil dead. They'll conclude that a third person had to have been involved, and then they'll be looking for me. They'll be looking all over for me.

I put the car in reverse, and then I'm gone. I drive and drive and drive until I see an exit I don't recognize. I get off the highway, and I drive until there are no houses on either side of me. I lie down in the back seat of my shitty Honda on the side of the road. I think about how hard it's going to be to sleep without my best friend.

Dahlia was the best friend I ever had. She was the only person I ever met like me. She was the only person who I ever felt saw me. She was so excited to live and be loved. I was so happy to love her. I wish I could have held her at the end, but I can only hope God's holding her now.

The next day I'm standing outside the car for an hour or two, just waiting to see the red and blue lights coming for me, but they never do. No one ever comes. No one ever calls. I resign myself to doing some of the drugs in the baggy. I take an Adderall while driving back to society, and I find that it's all still here.

Dahlia died, and the world didn't stop and say a prayer. Maybe no one will ever come for me. Perhaps it's not that I'll escape the law as much as that there isn't a law. The world's law is that even if someone reports you, you only get found if they care to see you.

But what if no one ever rushed into the hotel room? What if no one ever found their bodies? What if he was a cheating husband that did this all the time, so when his wife couldn't find him, she just left him and never looked back? Perhaps no one wants to disturb the rich people in those suites. It's possible that his credit card will just get charged every day he's there, and no one will ever ask questions.

I drive to an ATM to clean out his account, but the card is canceled. I try over and over, but it never works. I drive to another ATM and it's the same story. The pin number doesn't work, or she canceled the cards. If she canceled the cards, she might know he was murdered.

I have a miniature panic about this, but then realize that his wife could have closed the accounts to fuck her cheating husband over. I must have the wrong pin. Regardless, I cry and cry and cry and it doesn't change anything.

This was the worst robbery of my life. I earned one hundred dollars and a baggie of cheap drugs, and I lost the love of my life and the rest of my sanity.

I know my sanity is gone now because the only things I can think of are killing myself and returning to the casino to see if anyone has found them yet. The last place they would look for me by now would be at the casino itself. If I stay in the parking lot there for a couple nights and lay low, I'm sure no one will ever notice.

Yes, this is what I should do. I have to go back for her. I have to know what happened. She could be there, stumbling around, hopelessly lost. She could still be alive.

The sun goes down, the Addy kicks in hard, and my gas pedal hits the floor. I have nothing to live for, and I'm going back to see what kind of mess I've made. I look forward to pulling up. There she'll be. Dahlia in her beautiful dress. She'll smile and get in my car, and we'll kiss and giggle because we're crazy. But we're each other's kind of crazy. We never have to be alone again, so long as we have each other.

16.

I've sat in the parking lot, and I've sat in the parking lot, and I've sat in the parking lot. Nothing productive. No cops, no ambulances. No screaming, no news. I wait three hours, and I never see a single cop. I imagine they came and went at some point. Open and shut, murder-suicide or something like that. The cops don't care when a trans woman is murdered, but they would care that a white man was.

I bite my lip hard all day, and the Adderall makes me grind my teeth constantly. After twenty more minutes of sitting and waiting, I decide to make a plan. I have one hundred dollars in my pocket.

I drive to the pawnshop down the road and find that it's about to close. I beg the employees to let me in; it'll just be a minute. They let me in, and I buy a knife for thirty dollars. I consider buying a gun, but I figure that will be too loud indoors, no matter what viruses are floating around. Besides, I want intimacy.

And then I put the knife in my pants, wipe all the blood from my face, and walk back into the casino where I committed murder.

Immediately through the doors, I find quiet. It's the usual bustle of a casino and nothing more. Pop music is on the speakers; folks are smiling and laughing. It's still paradise. Paradise never changes.

I walk around with my eyes to the floor, listening for anyone talking about the murders, but I overhear nothing. It's just the same conversation as always. ZZ Top is coming to town. Isn't that great news?

My skin gets clammy and cold. I realize no one has found

them. Their lifeless bodies are still up there. They're still lying on the bathroom floor where I left them. I haven't been caught yet. I exhale, and the pressure gets to me. All at once, I panic and feel nauseous, and oh my God, I mangled someone, and he's still there.

I could go see how they've taken to death. I could go see Dahlia.

Maybe she's alive now. Perhaps she's scared and looking for me. Maybe she woke up, realized she'd been raped, there's a corpse next to her, and I'm gone and… Panic grips me, and I can feel my body failing. I shake my head and calm my nausea and make a beeline to the elevator.

I can't stand this. I feel like everything is falling apart. The elevator rushes up, but the whole world stands still. My guts pull on me as I ascend, but I feel unable to be sick again. I haven't eaten in days. The physical reaction of my body is only gagging, producing nothing but phlegm. I used to be nervous about a girl.

The doors open, and I burst out like a bullet. I resist the gags until I get to the door, and there they overtake me. I stand gagging at the door, and I can't stop, and I can't get control of myself. I search my bag for his cards, and I find them, and then there are the two keys. I pull the one for the room and swipe it. I pull the door hinge and slam my shoulder into the door, but it doesn't move.

What the fuck?

What the fuck?

I swipe the key. I listen for a beep, and there's nothing.

I try the hinge, and there's nothing.

I swipe the key. I try the hinge.

I swipe the card. I listen for a beep.

I scream bloody murder and fall on my knees. I just yell and scream.

The elevator ride back down is a relieving one.

Something happened.

Someone lived.

Someone lived, and they checked out of the room. That's the only way that there could possibly be no cops here.

93

That's the only fucking way.

It had to be Dahlia.

It had to be.

The Devil couldn't even see or breathe.

He was inches from death. There's no way he...

I rush through the lobby and up to the concierge. I don't give a fuck if they catch me anymore. I don't give a fuck if I go to prison. I just want to see her face one more time. I don't care if it's dead and bloated and gross. I just want to see her.

I don't care if she's dead. I'll kiss her like she was alive. I think of those crime scene photos and the bodies I wish I could cuddle and hold. I wish I could hold hers.

"Hi," I say. "So I'm staying in the room on this card, but it doesn't work. Can I get another one?"

The early twenties, plucky little bitch behind the counter smiles and says, "Of course! Let me take care of that for you, ma'am."

I wait. I wait. I wait.

"I'm sorry, ma'am, the computer says that you checked out yesterday," she says and scrunches up her face.

"That's not possible!" I shout. "That's impossible because I'm *here*, aren't I?"

"Ma'am, I'm sorry, but there's nothing I can do about the keycard," she says. "The computer says the room's been checked out of. It's cleaned, and ready for another guest."

My mind is flooding with wicked thoughts. This doesn't make sense.

"Do you have a form of ID, ma'am?" the bitch says.

"Okay, I had some friends staying with me," I say. "Do you know where they could have gone?"

She looks at me with confusion, and I realize that this is an entirely pointless question. This hotel doesn't want to cause a scene, so they took care of it privately. The police are probably in and out, constantly picking up fresh new faces. This isn't new here. No one knows what the fuck I'm talking about.

Or maybe it didn't even happen at all. When I think back

94

on the last week I've had, it's a blur. I've been awake for most of it, and it's only been nightmarish. I met the love of my life and lost her the same week. I took a human life. Or did I? Have I completely lost my mind? Maybe Dahlia is still here somewhere. Perhaps I just ran away confused, and none of that ever happened at all.

"Ma'am, if you'd like, I can let you stay in that room another night," she says. "But if it's a larger issue, you'll have to speak to my manager."

I slap the cash down on the counter and say, "Same room?"

And then I'm in the elevator again, and I have a key that works, and I know she's in that room waiting for me. I don't care that they have my ID on file. I know she's hiding in the closet or under the bed and she's gonna jump out and surprise me. She'll know I was coming back for her. I promised her I'd always catch her when she falls, and I came back to catch her. I don't care what happens to me anymore. I just have to catch her.

17.

I stand parallel with the door, exhale big, swipe, and then I hear a little chime. I tug on the hinge and the door opens. I walk in, and it's as if from my purest nightmares. I am back in hell. The ornate tile ceiling. The bedroom where we sat and then she ran to the bathroom and…

I count my steps and dread what I might find. Each step takes me closer to Dahlia's fate and even worse.

I put my hand against the wall and peer inside the bathroom, but instead of blood, it's all clean.

I take the final step into the bathroom, and it's all gone.

The Red Devil is gone, but so is Dahlia, and so is all the blood.

I turn to the tile wall Dahlia slammed his head into, but it's perfect and spotless. You would never know that two people died here.

Maybe two people didn't die. One of them had to have left and checked out. It had to be Dahlia. She had to have left. She checked out and left, and that's it. She's gone, and I'll never be able to find her.

I will wait in this casino for the rest of my life, and maybe one day, she'll come back to this horrible place where the worst imaginable thing happened to her. Perhaps she'll come back, and she'll see me there waiting for her. She'll drop everything and rush to hug me and kiss me and tell me she loved me.

I remember the dream she had about the bridge. In the dream, it was me who left, and she waited an eternity for my return. It was a premonition of my leaving her there on the bathroom floor to die. I left her there to wait for me, and now she will remain forever somewhere else.

I never got to tell her I loved her. And I did. I loved her.

She has to be out there. No one is looking for her now. Maybe she'll find peace out there somewhere...

I look around, and the more I look, the less I see the truth in front of me. I only know the story I'm telling myself. Maybe this is just how I want to remember what happened. Or maybe it never happened at all, really.

I have to find evidence. I have to know I'm not crazy, and that this happened. I get on my hands and knees, and I search under the counters for tiny spots of blood.

I check the crown molding.

I check under the toilet seat.

I check the grout on the floor.

But no matter where I look, I see the same thing. It's as if it never happened at all.

I sit up and look around for any sign that my memory isn't deceiving me, but I can't find anything anywhere. She was never here.

He was never here.

I was never here.

But then I remember something—a small detail that could save my sanity. I rip open my bag and dump it out on the bathroom floor. I move everything around until I find the cards, and then there it is. The proof is in front of me. His name was Daniel Lorre, and I have his credit cards. The only other lead I have is his wife's room key. I float the idea that the key might still work, and her room would have some kind of clue in it.

I imagined Dahlia waking up on the floor, raped, getting up, and seeing the rapist dead on the ground. She threatened to kill his wife. If she wanted some vengeance, she would try to find his wife's room and kill her. Maybe she did. I leave my belongings in the room and grab the two keycards and head out the door.

I'm going down the elevator and rushing through hallways, and then I'm there. I'm standing at the door, I have the keycard in my hand, and I think about her being there. Maybe she's dead inside. Perhaps it's a bloodbath. Maybe she's gone, and this is nothing. Perhaps this is everything. I swipe the card and hear the beep and slam the door open.

The air conditioning hits me in the face. It's significantly colder here than in the rest of the hotel. The A/C is on full blast. I take my first couple of steps into the darkness, and it's quiet.

There are bags in a pile on the living room floor.

There are signs of life everywhere.

I hear the murmur of a voice and drop to the ground.

If I listen closely, I can hear the faint sound of a shower and someone singing to themselves. His wife never left. I listen for another voice, but I don't hear one. She's alone, and she's in the most vulnerable place.

I flick on the lights, and it looks identical to the suite that we shared for a couple of hours until Daniel's untimely demise. It almost scares me, and I can see myself killing Daniel from the third-person perspective. I make myself sick.

I rush down the hall quietly and check to be sure I'm entirely alone, and I am. She's the only one here, and she might have answers. I don't know what she could possibly tell me that could help, but I'll take any lead I can on what happened. And besides, Dahlia promised Daniel to kill her, and if Dahlia hasn't, then I might need to do it for her.

I pull the knife from my pants and open it. The blade is sharp and strong in my hands. I approach the bathroom door and listen. It's like something out of a movie: the stillness, her absolute inability to escape. I hate it; it's just too perfect. I stand at the door with my knife drawn, and something feels wrong about it. Part of me wonders if I should just try talking to her and asking. And really, what had she done to deserve such a fate? Her husband was a scumbag? That's hardly a crime; we did her a favor.

I think this is wrong, but then the water goes off, and I have to decide.

I hesitate and listen as she leaves the shower, takes a towel, dries herself, and then stands in silence at the mirror

98

doing God knows what. Fuck. Fuck.

The door hinge turns, and the door cracks enough for light to peek out. We lock eyes through the gap in the door, and I grip my knife with all my might. I pull the door open and throw myself through and on top of her. She's immediately shocked, screaming, and kicking, so I produce the knife and stick it to her neck. Tiny cuts start forming in her throat from her constant jerking around. She realizes the danger of moving her head and stares up at me.

"Who are you?" she screams. "What do you want?"

"Do you know where your husband is?" I ask.

"No, no, no," she pleads. "Danny fucking took off on me. I don't know where he is."

I consider whether I believe her, but I can't imagine someone like her lying at knifepoint. She's scared to death.

"Any idea where he might have been?" I persist.

"I don't know," she screams. She inhales gently to avoid the knife. "Danny was gone! Danny was gone when I woke up, and he didn't leave anything behind, I swear!"

I'm getting frustrated. I want her to give me something I can actually use, but there's nothing. Maybe their bodies disappeared, and no one will ever find them. Perhaps the casino buried them in the lake. Maybe there's so much death here to cover up that they keep a giant furnace lit all day just in case someone dies in their hotel room.

She closed his accounts.

She was the one that closed them.

It had to be her.

She's lying.

I force the knife into one of the ridges of her neck and pull towards me enough to show her I mean fucking business.

"Why did you cancel his cards then?" I shout into her face.

She throws her eyes on me, and her hair stands on end. All at once, she realizes that I am the reason she doesn't have a husband anymore. I'm the reason that she will sleep alone. I took her best friend like she took mine.

"He was a bastard, and I was done with him," she states. "How do you know that?"

I almost feel sorry for her. I do feel sorry for her to an extent. I barge into her room, hold a knife to her neck, and now I have to tell her the truth. This is how she has to hear about it. This is probably the worst moment of her life, and usually, the worst moment of your life is followed by the last moment.

"Because while you were sleeping," I spit, "He was raping my dead girlfriend. He was raping her lifeless body. Your dearest Danny was a necrophiliac right until I mangled him and tore out his eyes. I watched him die by my hand, and you know what I did?"

"Ya know what I said to him?" I ask.

She shakes her head, and tears roll everywhere, and she winces in pain.

"I said I was going to find you and cut your head off with a big knife." I grin and feel the demon taking me over. "And I don't break promises."

She is not fond of this news. She violently contorts and tries to ignore the knife cutting the skin of her neck. She doesn't make much progress and falls limp again and starts shrieking and screaming for help. The screaming becomes that fight or flight screaming that really bothers the conscious. I power through as much screaming as possible, but it's too much, and I start to feel sick. I hate what I have to do.

Rabbits never make a sound until they die, and then they scream and scream.

"Shut the fuck up," I push. "I don't want to kill you yet. I want you to tell me something that helps me. I might let you live if you can give me information. How does that sound?"

But she's still screaming. I killed her husband, and there's nothing she can do. She's going to die just like he did, on identical tiles a couple of floors away.

"Bitch, I don't want to kill you." I cut into her neck meat just a touch to make her hear me.

"I don't want to die!" she screams. "I don't want to die.

Please. I don't want to die. Don't hurt me. Don't. Please."

And then I get sick. My goddamn tube can never cooperate. I gag, and with each gag, I feel her gag under my knife. I can't possibly vomit anything anymore. I have vomited the contents of my stomach for days now, and I know it's only a spasm. I gag on her naked chest and spit phlegm and bile at her. I feel horrible about this, but there's no alternative.

She becomes a pimple that pops in all directions. All at once, the terror of death and the gagging make her gag, and then vomit. She's lying flat on the tile ground, so the vomit has nowhere to go. It stays in her mouth and runs down her face. The knife at her neck and the vomit make her choke. When she starts choking, she thinks I'm killing her, so she releases her bowels.

A puddle of pee forms around her. The smell of shit fills the room, and then I'm gagging again. She's gagging.

Quickly I turn her on her side, and she coughs up the vomit and then vomits more. I take the knife off her neck, and her hands get free and race up to her neck to put it back together. It's not bleeding mortally, just a little bit.

She realizes the opportunity for escape and tries to stand. She pulls her legs up and steadies herself with the counter. Her panic makes her frantic. She tries to run.

Upon standing, she takes one and then two steps, slips on the combination of her urine and vomit and crashes her face into the wall. Her body firms up and quakes.

It's catastrophic.

Her face explodes like a watermelon, flesh slamming into the wall with a thud. At first, she is silent and confused, just as shocked as I am.

Her face slides down the wall, and she slides across the floor, and it slowly tears the skin from her face, revealing muscle and bone. The left side of her face starts to pile up at the top of her skull, and then she lands. She twitches and screams, and her face on the left side is in shambles but remains attached. The flesh lays lifeless on her screaming face.

I gag reflexively at the gore. It's the most shocking injury I've ever seen, and I can't look at it. She keeps screaming, and I keep feeling my empathy return, and it makes me angrier. I have to kill her now just to take the pain away. I don't want to look, but I do.

She's a bloody, shitty mess, and her hands won't leave her injury. Her fingers examine the terrible damage, and she wails and wails.

Her fingers examine her eye socket and find it broken and destroyed.

Her nose is clean off of the cartilage and bone.

I close my eyes and carefully move to her side. I touch her shoulder, and she falls into me. She falls into my chest and cries and wails. Suddenly I've become her mother, and I'm walking her through the darkness to the end. If she was afraid of me before, she loves me now.

I raise the remains of her chin and look into her sobbing and screaming face, and I see that love. I can see that intimacy, and I feel something new. I lean down and kiss her forehead, and I pat her naked shoulder. I rub down her back, and I run a hand through her matted hair. I ignore her smell and finally realize that she has a beautiful body. She had a beautiful face before she destroyed it; it's such a shame.

I love her now because I'm taking care of her. I love her because it feels good to love something so hurt. But I don't think I could ever feel this love outside of right now. This love is only temporary. Nevertheless, it's love.

I kiss her screaming face so intimately. I produce the knife and show it to her, and she seems glad to see it. She wants me to plunge it into her heart or head or neck and let her fly free away from all this pain.

I lay her down on the mutilated ground, and she falls so gracefully, like a doll. I take my position on top of her, and she almost smiles as if she still had a real mouth. Then I realize what I've always known deep down: I really like pain. I love its intimacy. It's the only thing closer than love.

"I'm so sorry, darlin'," I say. "But there's nothing we can do now."

She nods and tries to produce tears but then is just shaking and lying loosely.

"But if you want me to," I say. "I can make it painless, and you can just slip away."

Her eyes plead with me to give her that. She's ready for it. She contorts her lips into words.

"Please," she whispers.

But I'm not going to do that. I'm going to torture her for my own amusement. That's how I show my love. I have to tease her before giving her what she wants, or she won't enjoy it.

I lean down, and I say, "I know you really want this, but we have a little more to do."

I've always wanted to know how much someone could sustain. I've always wanted to see how a person looks without any limbs. Am I trying to distract myself from the pain I feel about Dahlia? Is this wrong? I've always wanted to hold someone's insides while they were alive.

"I can teach you how to like it," I say.

PART III: DEVOUR

18.

I'm nothing.
There's nothing.
I'm nowhere.
It's all gone now.
Bliss and peace are here.

The great thing about alcohol sleep is that you don't dream. You fall into this beautiful dark pit of the abyss where all the souls collect before annihilation or reincarnation. I'm there. I'm in the hole, and I'm prepared for destruction, and I don't care.

I want to go.

There are several others here in the pit with me.

There's a teenage prostitute.

There's a gambler in over his head.

Then there's a man who I catch looking at me without eyes.

He stares into me, and I feel the intense sense that I know him. I try to swim over to him in this spaceless place, but he gets farther away as I get closer. I keep swimming, and he keeps looking, and the darkness keeps approaching, and suddenly he is covered by darkness and gone. Annihilation or reincarnation? I look at God and ask.

Then the darkness recedes, and I see the all too familiar bubbles of so many annihilated before him. He's gone, and his soul was not spared. God is just. I swim over to God and look upon it, and it's beautiful. A huge shining light in the center of the sky, and I can hear voices inside if I listen hard.

I'm ready for my light to dim too.

I don't want to be reincarnated.

I don't want to be a baby again.

I want to be nothing.

I want to be nothing!

God descends to me, and I look up at it, and I smile a celestial smile. Oh my God, I want to be nothing! I want to be nothing!! The concept excites my little soul, and I flutter, and then it's time.

God smiles down on me and extends a celestial arm to me. It's sharp, and I feel it pierce me, and then it starts to burn. I feel this burning take over my whole soul, and I realize that this is it! Annihilation! I am at peace. I love the burning. It is the most fantastic burning.

God lifts its hand once and then slams into me again. I'm pierced again, and the burning takes over my senses, and then all I feel is the burning.

I am on fire.

I am my mom.

I am on fire like my mom was.

I was a baby, and my mother had me with the intention of saving herself from loneliness, and I set her on fire. I did. I set her on fire, and now I burn with her.

God raises its hand again and then comes down, and a beam of light fires out of my soul. But instead of disintegration and dissolving into nothingness, I burst outward, and I glow. I shine and burn, and my being heals, and the burning becomes the feeling of love. The love of the universe holds me in its invisible little hand.

Reincarnation! Shit! No! No! God, please. Don't put me back. I can't go back. I can't do it again. I can't keep doing this. Please. I just want to die. Please, just let me go back home. I want there to be nothing. I don't want to see. I don't want to hear. I want to exhale and be silent. I want my silence.

But then I get the silence I want. All is black and dark, and God has abandoned me. I am alone. My body starts to materialize around me. My left arm and torso regenerate, then my face and my legs. I turn my face and see a giant spear sticking out of the earth where my right arm should be, and I realize that it didn't regenerate with the rest of me.

I grip my left arm, and the nerves kick back to life, and I can feel again. I can feel every part of me. I can feel my soul return to its home, and I launch awake. Immediately, I am overtaken by the worst pain I've ever experienced. When you've genuinely been under and in that place without pain, the human body becomes a challenge to pilot. I sit up and look at the spear, and it takes further shape. It's a shovel, and it's stuck in the dirt. Then I see it. My arm is lying next to it, which means it's not attached to me. I evaluate my wrist and notice that I have a bloody wound where my forearm starts.

I look around in agony and only see blackness. I put my hand out, and I feel the familiar crumbing of dirt and rocks. I try to stand myself up and fall back down. I try to get a grip on soil and roots, and again I fail. Each fall takes the wind out of me, and I regain my bearings and try again. I grab a root and catch one. My body lifts and floats, and then I'm nearly standing.

The blood drains out of my arm, and the pain is so intense that I bite my lip and draw blood, but the pain doesn't stop. I lift my hand up, find grass and dirt, and realize I'm in a big hole. My arm is hopeless. I can't just climb out. I kick my bare feet into the dirt and make a slot for them to sit. I prop myself up and look out of the hole. I'm in a secluded garden area of a high-rise building. I'm on the ground, and the building is gargantuan above me. Why am I here?

I reach out of the hole and find another root. I grip it, kick off and pull, and my body slides across the grass and out of my premature grave. I pant and pant and wail in pain. I lie on my back, and the building towers over me. I have to keep moving.

I sit up, and I get a better grasp of my environment. I'm in the courtyard of the fanciest hotel I've ever seen. There are seven holes in the ground. Most of them are full of dirt, with a bit of plant coming out of the top. I can't help but identify that my hole is partially filled in. I get a mental image of what could have happened.

Someone was trying to bury me and six others. When

they got to me, they must have hit me with the shovel and thought I moved. So, then they struck me to see if I'd move, and it took a while, but eventually, my arm came off, and I woke back up. Any minute, someone will return to deal with me. I have to find a way out of here.

Why would someone want to bury me?

19.

I'm good at this. I'm really good at this. I drag the knife across the skin on her wrist, and then I press down with all my might. The blade sinks into flesh, and her broken vocal cords call out. But no one can hear her, and there's not much left to save.

The knife carves gently and cleanly through arteries and nerves. It takes a lot of effort, but I'm able to break her bones. She howls and howls, and I feel oddly mesmerized. After a point, I'm just enjoying myself. I'm not scared anymore. I'm not gagging anymore. I'm good at this, and I'm focused.

At long last, her hand detaches at the forearm, and she sighs with relief. The hardest part of pain is the pressure, but once the pressure is over, you just need to evaluate what you've lost. I bend down and lift the separated hand, and I feel pride. I doubt many women in the world could say they've done this. Maybe more than I'd care to think. I don't care if my parents are disappointed. I don't care if Dahlia is dead. At this moment, I love pain more than any of that.

Words become impossible for her. Her experience is without any accurate description anyway, so I don't blame her for just screaming. I want to ask her about what she likes. I want to talk to her about what turns her on, but I can't disturb her experience. And I don't want to care anyways. I don't want anything other than her body; her soul is useless to me.

I've grown so tired of love. Over and over, I put my all into someone, and I say that they're special. We fall in again and out again, like straight people sex. So predictable.

I say that they could be the love of my life.

I say they could save me from some anonymous villain.

But the truth is, I love myself. I have always loved myself. I don't need love because I don't have an anonymous villain, and I don't need rescuing.

I can fend for myself.

I am the villain.

I wear the black hat with pride.

I don't need anything but myself.

I show her the hand, and she whimpers and squints, but the blood and vomit have made it so difficult to see. I wipe her eye and try to show her again, but she just vomits hoarsely. I'm so disappointed. She has so much to learn.

I'm so tired of love because it isn't close enough. I deserve more than anyone can give me.

I deserve everything.

I deserve the end.

I deserve their demise.

If someone loves me, they'll give me that willingly. When someone dies for me, and they beg me for it, then I'll know they love me.

Her arm bleeds way more than I'm ready to handle, and I can see that my fun won't last much longer. She's going to finish without me. I will have to hurry if I want to show her what else I can do. I get an idea and think, yes, she's going to love this.

I toss her hand away and sit up on top of her. I inch backward and find a beautiful crevice about her navel. I lean down and gently kiss it up and down. I feel all the tiny hairs stand on end, and I know she likes me. She loves me. She's going to fall for me.

I lick down her navel and find her pubic hair. It's cute. She's done shaping to make it more appealing, but it remains a sexual organ and nothing more. It's a pity no one will ever fuck her now. It's a shame that she'll never get to use her freshly manicured pussy on some new anonymous hopeful man to replace her dead husband. Maybe she's a secret lesbian too.

Maybe she's a secret lesbian too. The thought lingers, and I run my fingers through her pubic hair. I'm getting distracted. I find the gentle indent in her navel and I place the knife at its crease. I sit up and look to what's left of her face for approval, and I find it.

Her screams sound like sighs.

Her pain sounds like pleasure.

We've made it.

I push the knife into her navel, and it squishes through with ease. She arches her back, and I can see she's right on edge. I pull the blade gently down her stomach and make a beautiful little tear. She calls out for me in euphoria, and I feel her drain under me. I turn my head to look at her legs and find she's relieved herself again.

I pull out the knife and put it in my back pocket. I place my fingers on either side of the wound and enjoy its titillation. She can barely contain herself from all the pleasure, so I push my fingers up, and then I'm rubbing her wound up and down. With my right hand, I check to see her response when I slip inside. She doesn't feel me enter at first, but then my fingers are inside her, and I can handle all of her miracles.

I feel the marvelous display of tubes and pipes and warmth and know that it's home. Someone could live here and grow up here within these pipes. The miracle of life at my fingertips. The slickness makes all of her tubes challenging to grasp. I consider showing her this miracle too, but then I remember my ethics. This is not about her. This is about my experience, my pleasure, my enjoyment.

I remove my hand from her holy site, and it's covered in a mass of goo. I wipe it on my shirt and proceed down her body. Her screams become coos of delight with every touch and every sensation. I run down her pubic hair again, and I think of our poor host. If I let her go, no one will ever want to touch her again. She will treasure her perfect pussy for private use. I imagine her masturbating years later without a face.

This is so sad.

I can't allow this.

I lower my fingers and succumb to her desires.

She reacts with glee and panic.

She loves it and has always wanted this and has never known how to ask another woman.

I can do it for you.

I run my fingers down her labia and tease her, but she knows what I want to do. I climb myself off of her and pull her legs apart. She gets nervous and tries to keep them closed, but I'm persistent. You have to force people to get what they want.

I push my lips up to her vagina, and then I'm eating it. With my tongue, I quickly locate her clit and hood. I lick around the hood, and she coos with delight. I feel like doing everything to her that I've ever wished someone would do for me. Then I realize the most profound connection we share.

Deep down, we both just want to die now. I want to die because my life is a monotonous cycle of falling in and out of love. She wants to die because no one will ever love her again. We're a match made in hell. I must do for her what I wish someone would do for me. It's not about her pleasure at all! It's about mine. It feels good to watch her die and know that I killed her. No matter who it is, that's power.

I could kill anyone I wanted. I could kill everyone. I could destroy the world. Only then will I allow myself to die.

I take the knife back out of my pocket, and I open it. I remove my face from her vagina and peer down at it. She's had her lesbian experience, and that's great for her. But what do I want? The only thing pretty about her now is her pussy. I shove the knife up to her labia and she mutters.

"Please…" she begs. "Please, just kill me. I wanna die! I wanna die! This can't be real! I wanna die!"

That's more like it. Now cum for me.

I rip at her vagina with the knife, and with my other hand, I'm able to get a grip. She screams from her guts, and it bellows through the room. I squeeze and pull to get leverage, and eventually, the knife makes some progress. With the last of her life, she's scrambling her legs around so much that it's difficult, but finally, I see the knife cutting through her clitoris. Yes. Yes.

She scrambles and scrambles, but it's a no-go. Her clitoris comes off with ease, and she screams from the bottom of her lungs. She instantly starts urinating and shitting and shaking violently. She spasms so hard that I let go of her vagina. I look down, and I'm holding her labia and clit in my hands.

Wow. It's amazing. I cringe with my entire body. It's the most unbelievable pain I can imagine causing and watching her suffer makes me suffer too. I feel such a lovely pain. I watch her squirm in shock, and I think the same way. I know her pain, and I shake too. I fall onto the floor and shake and scream with her. We're together in this.

She quakes like a chicken with its head cut off. I can't hold her down enough, and she's unresponsive. Finally, I flip her back on her back. She's covered in bile and shit. She's just had the best orgasm of her life. It feels good to know I gave that to her. I look at her mutilated remains, and I ask myself about love. Now that I've given all the love I have, I get to enjoy some in return.

I slide myself on top of her and push her blown-out face to the side. She's still breathing, but only barely. Her legs randomly kick. I push the knife up to the side of her neck and she exhales. I catch her eye, and it still gently flutters around in her head.

"Thank you," I say. "You're the best I've ever had."

And then I pull her hair towards the blade and the blade the opposite way. The knife is dulling but still manages to break through flesh and then vein, and then she squirts blood all over the ground. It's more blood than I've ever seen, and again, I'm overcome with gagging. Her throat gurgles, choking on the blood. I have to finish. I grip the knife and pull, and even more blood sprays out. It sprays on my face and hers, and I think, wow, she's really cumming.

I rip through her throat to the other side. Then I fall down in exhaustion. All I hear now is silence. I look up at the

113

ornate ceiling, somehow covered in blood. I lean my head back and cuddle between her knees. I find her clit, and I kiss it. It belonged to a woman I loved. But this time, it didn't end because I fucked something up.

It didn't end because I was too emotional.

It didn't end because I was too clingy.

It didn't end because she found someone better.

She didn't move away.

She didn't tell me she was actually straight, and this was just a phase.

She didn't say I wasn't sexual enough.

She didn't hurt me.

She gave and gave and gave until there was nothing left.

I loved a woman to completion. This proves that I know how.

All love ends. It's inevitable. I think the inevitability of its demise makes people do crazy things to each other. We get so scared that our lover will leave us or hurt us, but in the end, that pales in comparison to what death can do. Love and its demise go hand in hand. We always lose the ones we love. Always.

But tonight, I loved a woman to completion.

20.

It's so dark, and I'm bleeding everywhere, but I duck through halls and turn my arm to my chest and try to keep my ripped dress together. I start to cry and get overwhelmed and then find a little corner in the darkness. I fall to my knees, and I hold myself with one arm, and I just cry.

I cry and cry and cry.

I cry about being alive.

I'm lost.

I need someone to find me.

Who am I?

Where am I?

What's happening to me?

Why am I even alive?

Baby's first panic attack.

I set my mom on fire. That's right, I dumped gasoline on her and burned her. I burned her alive with fire on my front lawn. I got so sick of her shit that I burned her like a monk.

I did it to impress a girl. I'm actually timid and lonely. I don't talk to people or look at them if I can help it. If there's one thing I know down to my core, it's that people are cruel, and their cruelty is something I must defend against at all costs. I can't ever open myself up again. All I know is that I can't be cruel to myself. I have to protect my vitality at all costs.

I stand back up and look around the corner. No one is here, and all is quiet. I keep walking until I find an exit door, and then I'm in a massive parking lot. I've lost a lot of blood, and I'm getting dizzy. I crash on the curb and lie down and get my first honest look at the night sky.

It's incredible up there tonight. My celestial home is with me now, and I feel more at peace with myself. I am a cosmic being from space sent here to experience this earth's love, growth, and beauty. I should consider myself the luckiest.

I'm in the parking lot of a casino, and that's weird. I remember those television spots I saw growing up about gambling addiction and people addicted to risk. They always ended with some guy getting buried in the desert on TV. Then I laugh.

I must be in the body of some silly bitch with a gambling addiction. I must have hopped into this body right at the last second before they buried her for good. Oh my God! I imagine the burial crew returning to my gravesite and seeing nothing but my arm. They know I climbed out, and they're imagining I'm coming to get them. Maybe I should, I think and laugh. Perhaps I should pretend to haunt this casino and jump out and scare people with my one arm and my deathlike appearance.

I stand and cover myself as best I can and walk through the side door of the casino. I find a scarf blowing in the wind and grab it and tie off my arm. I need food and water and a bathroom. I need to reenter society and see if I can get some shelter until I figure out my purpose.

Immediately, I hear pop music blaring from the speakers. I smell the faint smell of one million dead cigarettes. My eyes circle the room. I see a couple of tourists poring over their phones, and I stop worrying. I walk across the room and move deeper into the casino. Then I'm in a massive room with a million slot machines all ringing at once. I walk through the aisles, and I find a drink station. You can have an unlimited quantity of whatever drink you want. So I take a cup and fill it with water. I fill it twice and three times and again and again until I've filled myself.

I turn and immediately see a bathroom sign. I approach with caution and purpose, but find I'm given no resistance. I enter the bathroom quietly and grab the first stall I can. I sit down and only just notice the air conditioning and suddenly feel amazing. The lack of blood and abundance of water clench together, and I urinate. It's amazing. I feel a sense of total physical relief and centeredness. I lay my head against the tile wall, and I find myself dozing, nearly asleep from blood loss and comfort.

It's not enough to kill me. I shake it off, flush and stand.

I step out of the stall and drag my hand across the wall for balance.

Things are getting progressively more surreal.

Colors are intensifying and blurring and leaving a black trail.

I see tiny rocket ships in my vision, and they explode into stars. I feel myself slipping and shake it off.

I come crashing into the sink, and I finally get a look at myself in the mirror. I am covered in dirt and caked blood. I couldn't possibly fool anyone. I was a corpse. I died and came back from the dead. My skin is pale as a sheet, and my eyes lack any color. I imagine that this is how vampires feel. Or maybe this is what demonic possession is like.

I came into this poor girl's body and just look at her. This is so sad. I fill my remaining hand with water and splash it on my face, but it doesn't disguise any of my problems. When I return to Earth, it is as the dead. I can't change this about myself, but I can be happy that I made it. I catch myself smiling and see the beauty underneath the dirt. I knew she was in there somewhere.

I hear the noise of the door opening, and I know that I'm caught. Someone will walk in, take one look at me, and know they've seen a ghost. I can't hide my death-like appearance. I consider running to a stall, but I feel my own weaknesses. I decide to hold my face to the corner so it can't be seen.

But then my eye deceives me and crawls to the corner of its socket to view my threat. The woman enters slowly, taking in every inch of the bathroom. She feels hesitation when she sees me and straightens herself. She's beautiful. She's wearing a black silk dress that extends to her ankles.

Her makeup is lavish and elegant, but subtle and demure.

She smells immaculate, like an expensive perfume.

She is expensive.

I throw my eye back to the corner, and then I hear a voice.

"Baby doll," she says. "Honey, are you okay?"

I don't want her to be talking to me. I really don't want her to be talking to me.

But she is.

She's talking to me.

I can't avoid my face.

I can't avoid my voice.

Do I still have a voice?

Can I still speak?

I don't know my name.

I don't know where I am.

I'm lost. I'm so hopelessly lost.

"Sweetheart," she pries and puts her hand on my shoulder. It's gentle. I flinch away, but find it motherly and soothing. I turn to face her in terror, but she doesn't shriek and run. She sees my ghostly appearance and she only says, "Oh my gosh, darling. We have got to get you cleaned up."

She doesn't notice my lack of an arm. Maybe she thinks I'm just on drugs or got beat up or something.

"What's your name, sugar?" she asks. I think about this, but I don't know my name. I don't know who I am. I don't know anything, and even if I did, I can't remember how to speak.

I just shake my head.

"Oh honey." She frowns. "Someone must have hurt you real bad, huh?"

Tears slip out of the corners of my eyes. I nod my head and whimper, and then my head is on her shoulder. She knows my pain. I cry and cry and cry and cry, and it feels like the most necessary cry of my whole life. I cry until I can't cry anymore, and I feel horrible about doing it on her expensive dress. But she doesn't care; she just holds me, runs her hand through my hair, and picks out matted pieces.

"We should get you some water," she says. "I'll bet you haven't eaten today, have you?"

I shake my head on her shoulder, no doubt wiping tears,

snot, and dirt all over her.

"Okay, let's get you cleaned up," she says. "Then let's take you over to the diner and get you a nice stack of pancakes and a couple eggs. That should fix you right up, and then you can tell me what happened."

Okay, momma. The more she speaks, the calmer I get, and I feel my body loosen. She reaches into her purse and produces a handkerchief. She wets it and starts scraping dirt and blood off my face.

"I'm sorry, darling," she says with a distinct drawl. "I don't want to hurt you, but I know you want me to get all this off of you."

And I do.

The pain doesn't hurt me anymore.

She's putting me back together piece by painful piece.

When the time comes, and I can't stand it anymore, I'll show her my arm. She'll want to immediately take me to the hospital, but I know this is where I belong for now. I know this is the place I'm meant to be. I was sent here by God to be right here. I can't let her stop me.

She decides to give up on my face after the handkerchief gets too dirty to continue. She holds my chin between her fingers, and she turns me to face myself. In the mirror, I see the most beautiful girl I've ever seen. Her eyes no longer carry the darkness. Her face glows, and her face is my face. I know a demon cannot fall in love with their vessel, but I feel love and pride in who I am. I feel the beauty of seeing myself for the first time, and it overcomes me.

I shift back to the woman, and I love her. I look at her and mouth the words "How can I thank you?" and cry and cry.

She says, "I can't *hear* you, baby girl."

I can't talk.

"Okay, if you don't have a name, then I'm gonna call you Chelsea until you remember. Chelsea's my daughter's name. Let's take you over to the diner and get you fed."

Then she holds my hand and walks me out of the bathroom, and the world feels different to me. The bathroom gives birth to me, and now I'm alive again. I look around the casino and see a safe home of LEDs and screaming alarms. The woman drags me through the casino as quickly as she can while avoiding any people she sees.

I don't feel the urge to look down at all anymore. I look up and around, and I am all at once united with my fellow creatures. I'm a part of the club now. I am no different from every old woman here begging God to let her get lucky. Just let tonight be the night I hit it big. And then I know my purpose. I'm not meant to lead anything at all but to play a role. I can pick a hat and put it on and become that person. I can be anyone I want. I can be anything I want. But I'm so glad that I'm me. I was brought back to life to be part of the world for the first time.

The woman drags me into the diner next to the poker tables, and we rush to a booth. She assures me that she can take care of everything, and I don't need to worry about anything. All I need to do is be here and stay alive and be a part of the world. All I need to do is be a girl. I'm so lucky to be a girl.

"Let's get some water and some pancakes and some eggs for my daughter, Chelsea, here," she says, making direct eye contact with the waitress. "Just bring me a cup of coffee."

I smile with my new face. I smile, and it doesn't hurt my face to smile. It feels like Heaven to smile. It feels like permission.

I look around and see such life.

A couple sits smoking cigarettes and grunting about losses.

A man sits alone and texts his son for the first time this year.

A woman breaks up with her boyfriend so she can explore her options.

A guy has a cigarette, and that makes him content enough to keep moving today.

There is a wave of love and understanding, and I feel my remaining hand reach down to the upholstered booth, and the booth grows a hand, and that hand holds mine, and it's so warm. I feel the ground turn into one million tiny palms, and they all hold me up so I don't fall into the Earth. The

Earth is a big hand, and it's made for me to dance within. I have to dance upon the great palm. Life is about finding a way to dance upon the great palm.

The profundity of my existence overwhelms me, and I start sobbing again. I look around, and I see colors, and I know they're a miracle just like me, and it makes me cry even harder. I see a woman smoking her cigarette and drinking her coffee and pushing coins into a machine, and behind her eyes, I see a little consciousness like mine. A beautiful tiny organism is taken in by lights and sounds, and colors.

But then I realize that my mother is the most authentic love of all, and I turn to her, and my God, she's perfect. I look into her like I've looked into so many others, and I see a radiant light inside her blue eyes.

I can see her whole life.

She was a little girl, just like I was.

She was dating a boy.

She failed a test, and it ruined her life.

She ripped holes in her pants and got in trouble.

She kissed a girl once, and she never recovered.

She had a little girl; she experienced the beauty of birth. The miracle of life is something she's capable of, and I can see her performing the miracle on me.

The food and water come, and I'm scared to try it. I reach my hand out for the water, but then the crystal droplets on the outside speak to me and say that it's okay. I grip the cold water, and my body is enveloped in an icy chill. I put it to my lips, and the water slips down the back of my throat, and then I feel my stomach grow colder, and I smile. Water is a miracle too.

The food is warm when it touches my lips and then my tongue. I slosh around eggs and swallow, and my body fills with relief and peace. It's the most glorious meal I've ever had, and I look at the woman who saved me, and again, I mouth the words "thank you." And she just smiles and watches me eat and knows she's done her saintly duty for the day.

God sent me an angel.

21.

The pancakes melt in my mouth like butter on my tongue. The sweet and doughy flavor activates a part of my brain that I didn't know I had. I feel awake again. I feel alive again. My blood sugar starts to stabilize, and my salt cravings are satiated. I am hydrated.

"So what happened to you?" she pries. "Do you speak English at all? Can you even make a noise?"

I don't remember how to make noises with my throat. But then I remember the scream that I could belt. I remember how to produce some sound. I grunt from the back of my throat, and she smiles.

"Okay, can you hum, sweetie?" she asks. "Try doing this."

She hums a little song, and I think I've heard it before. It's a song I used to hear in music class when I was a little kid. I try to vibrate my head, and then I can. I find myself purring like a cat, and then she nods and encourages me to make the vibrations come forward in my mouth. I vibrate my teeth and the tip of my tongue, and then I can do it without effort.

"Very good!" she says. "All right, now here's the tricky part. You have to do that with your mouth open. Just remember that you want to speak so that your lips vibrate."

I need to make my lips vibrate with my mouth open. I open my mouth and make a sound and then migrate that sound to the tip of my tongue.

"Yes!" she says. "Now use your lips to form the words you want to say, and then just make the tip of your tongue, and your teeth, and your lips vibrate when you form the words. I want you to say, 'Happy birthday!' Can you say 'happy birthday' for me?"

I stare into the table, and I reach inside myself to find the voice that I must have. I quickly formulate the plan and mouth the words "Happy birthday." Then I make the sound with my throat and move it to my lips. Then with the sound there, I mouth "Happy birthday," and then I'm just saying it.

"Baby, I'm so proud of you," she says and weeps. She is proud of me. I can feel that pride and love. I feel like I could be her daughter forever. I wish I had a mom like this and not the one I set on fire. I'd never set her on fire. She is perfect, and I owe her my life.

"Happy birthday!" I shout. "Happy birthday!"

"Now, can you try to tell me your *name*?" she asks and stares into me.

I find the sound and bring it to my lips and form the word.

"Chelsea!" I say and smile.

She starts laughing, and I start laughing, and then I'm happy. Happiness is a new feeling. It's impossible to feel pleased with your guard up. But once I let my guard down and let myself go, I feel the happiness flow through me, and I know the joy of being alive. I laugh harder and harder.

"Well, okay, Chelsea," she smiles. "What happened to you? Can you tell me anything you remember?"

I think really hard back to all the things I remember. It's a genuine struggle. I only remember certain pieces, and all of it is inconsequential to how I ended up here.

"Hole," I say. "Climbed."

She nods with a confused expression.

"Escape. Looking for help," I say. "You."

I point with my left hand at her and smile. She's what I remember. She's what I want to remember.

"Name?" I ask.

"My name is Stacy, sweetheart." She smiles warmly. With that, we're complete. She is Stacy, and I'm her daughter Chelsea, and we're a happy family. Maybe Chelsea wasn't even real at all, and she just wanted a daughter. Maybe Stacy always wanted a daughter, and now she's found one. Maybe Stacy needs me as much as I need her. I love my mom.

"Stacy," I say and point. She nods, and I start crying again. I'm so happy.

Instinctively, I try to move my right arm to grab the tears from my eyes but find that it doesn't exist. I'm confused, but then I remember that I only have one hand now. I think about my right arm and if I'm going to miss it. The truth is, I don't have any memories of having a right arm, so I guess I never really needed it after all.

"Chelsea, sweetie," she says. "I know we just met, but if you trust me, I know a place where you can have a shower, and maybe we can get you more cleaned up and in some different clothes. How does that sound?"

I have been holding my dress closed the entire evening with either my hand or my legs. I feel the dirt and blood and pressure on my body and know I need to clean myself. I haven't given my body much thought or even evaluated if it was hurt. I knew I could walk, and now I know I can talk. As long as I could do those things, I figured I would be okay. Although sitting on the upholstery gives me a pain I can't shake in my lower abdomen. It grows by the minute, and now that I've acknowledged it, the floodgate opens wide.

I nod my head and throw my left arm around my stomach. I cringe inwardly and feel air escape my ass with little effort. With the air comes a wave of intense burning, and I can barely breathe. I gasp and gasp, and gasp, and then Stacy shouts, "Baby, what's wrong? Baby, just slow your breathing. It's okay. I've got you. Let's get you out of here and let's get you cleaned up."

She comes around the booth, pulls my left arm from around my stomach, and lifts me to my feet. I gather my bones toward the earth, and I feel the pressure building in my abdomen. She throws an arm around my shoulder, and I wince with pain. I take one step with her and then two, and then I find I can walk without doubling over. I walk independently for a moment while Stacy pays for the food and coffee. She guides me over to an elevator, and I walk with her, wincing at every step.

Now we're in the elevator, racing into the sky, and the

pressure pulls air out of my abdomen, and I feel wetness around my ass. I know something is wrong with my body, and I can't afford to let myself get hurt. I have to stay alive; I have to be healthy. I hold on as hard as I can. Stacy is trying to hold me up. The elevator doors open, and we shoot out and race towards a numbered entryway. She flicks the keycard, yanks on the handle, and the door opens.

The A/C hits me in the face, and it's colder than the rest of the hotel by a noticeable margin. I shiver and step inside. Bags are lying scattered over the floor, ripped open. I ease my way in and lie on the couch. Stacy races to my side and bends down.

"Honey, do you wanna get these clothes off while I get you a towel?" she asks. I nod and she stands. I can't imagine being naked in front of her, but I guess she is my mom. I need to let her take care of me.

She looks down at me for a minute and does a 'go ahead' motion with her hand. I let the rip in my dress go, and the dress spreads up my leg and thigh. Immediately, I see my legs are covered in blood. She cringes and scowls and runs away to get a towel.

I pull the tail of the dress up over my waist and to my breasts. I know it's going to hurt when I get it off around my arm. I know she's going to find my arm like this, and it's all going to end. But maybe it should. Maybe I should let a medical professional save my life. That's my purpose, after all, to be alive and to live. I pull the dress over my shoulder and lift my half-arm. I scream and shout, but I pull with all my might, and the dress comes off over my head. I lower my arms and throw the dress aside, and pant.

I look down at my body, and it's a bloody, bruised disaster. It's caked with so much blackness that it's nearly impossible to identify anything below my belly button. I slip my left hand down my body, and it hurts all over. I ease my fingers into my caked and bloody pubic hair, and it's thick with pain and substances. But then I find flesh, and then I panic when I realize I have a penis.

Stacy comes rushing into the room as I make this

realization and shouts, "Is everything alright, darling?"

Then she sees me. She really sees me. I am a bloody, disgusting wreck. I have one arm. I have a penis, and I'm a girl, and I have one arm, and I'm beautiful, and I'm destroyed. Someone hurt me really bad. Once upon a time, someone hurt me really bad.

22.

Today is a day of marvelous firsts. I've never gone on a first date with a girl twice in one week before. But here we are, and I'm Stacy. She's my daughter Chelsea, and I love her, and now she's in my dearly departed one-night-stand's hotel suite, and we're alone. We're mother and daughter, and I'm gonna take care of her.

Flashback to when I was ripping this room apart a couple of hours ago to find the most expensive shit this bitch had.

I put on all her favorite things.

I became her.

I wore her makeup.

I wore her perfume.

I knew this was the best way to carry out the rest of my earthly plans. I would need to lead more up to this room and see just how many I could pile up in the corner before someone came in shooting. I knew it would never happen. This hotel is a beautiful place where no one ever dies, and if I pile the bodies up, the cleaning crew will just handle my crimes for me.

I went to the bar to prowl around, and there he was. Lucky guy number two. I decided killing guys and stealing their drugs would be much easier without assistance. I was alone, and I was unstoppable. I had killed many now and knew I could quickly kill again.

His name is Ethan—isn't that sweet. I slipped him a cocktail napkin with a room number and a time on it and winked my sinister wink. He flashed one back after he read the napkin, and I knew he meant business. I figured I deserved one more fun night on the house before hopping out of here and finding a new base of operations.

So, I gave little Ethan the napkin, and he winked, and then I ran off to the bathroom to celebrate with a line of coke, courtesy of Daniel.

Thank you, Danny.

But then I walked into the bathroom, and I saw a fucking ghost. I genuinely thought she was a ghost. I thought she was back to haunt me for cheating on her or something. But then I realized she was hiding from me.

I thought about saying, "Dahlia?" Then I got too scared. I approached with caution. But guess what? She didn't even see me correctly. I can see in her eyes that she's a blank slate. She was reborn through her little trauma, and now she's this other person. I know I could never love Dahlia again; I grieved her loss and moved on.

But this isn't Dahlia.

This is someone else.

This is my favorite thing in the whole world.

She was a lost girl who didn't know what she wanted. All at once, I knew I could show her. I could show her what she wanted. We didn't have to talk about the rape, and we didn't need to rush into a relationship. We just needed to talk. I taught her how to speak. I fed her. We laughed, and it was just like before. It was like when Dahlia and I were close, but it was better now. I was an independent woman; I didn't need her anymore. And she was a new person, and she didn't understand her needs, and then suddenly we were better. We were better than ever before.

I know that I don't want to put labels on things, but I can feel myself falling in love with her all over again. But now she's Chelsea. She's my daughter, and I love her like a mother loves a daughter. I have to protect her. I have to save her. I have to teach her. I have to clean her.

So I bring her to the room, and she takes off her dress, and I see that things are worse than I could have imagined. Her body is a disaster. Her right arm is snapped off like a branch from a tree. I feel her agony, and it makes me nearly double over with euphoria. She has suffered more than

128

anyone I could ever imagine, and yet she's still here, and she's still perfect, and she's my daughter. She's my beautiful daughter, and this time I got to name her. My baby Chelsea.

I take the towel and drape it over her body, and she looks up at me with love. I tuck her in and say, "Does the baby want to take a shower?" And she nods.

"Okay, sweetheart, but you've gotta keep your eyes closed until we get in the shower." I feel myself grin. "Okay?"

She smiles and knows that it's just a game between mother and daughter. A secret between us.

"If you want, I can join you and help you get clean," and now I'm getting wet. I want to clean every part of her, but I also want to see all her damage. I want to be the one to inspect her pain. I want to secure her away from all the pain I haven't caused her. She's all for me now.

She nods and smiles, and then I have her in my arms. And I say, "Close your eyes, little one," and she does. I kiss her on her forehead. I carry her through the bloody hallway and push open the bathroom door. I take one careful barefoot step around the blood and vomit to another available spot and another.

"Keep 'em closed, sweetheart," I reiterate. I step over the body of Miss Dearly Departed, or what's left of her.

I take her into the shower, and the water is on and waiting for her.

I lay her in the rain, and she sighs with her eyes closed.

I close the shower door, and then she's gone.

I sigh and look around, knowing that this could be a problem. Ethan is coming at two in the morning, and Chelsea is here now, which is inconvenient.

"Smell," I hear Chelsea shout in the shower, and I panic because I know what she's talking about. And at this moment, I remember the other hotel room I checked into today. It was the hotel room from earlier, all cleaned and sanitized. It's the perfect place to continue our festivities. I just need to move the whole party up there and leave this room behind. It's a shame because I really like the idea of using Miss Dearly Departed's body as a party favor, but the smell in here is only going to get worse.

"Chelsea baby," I shout. "The fucking toilet just backed up, and the whole bathroom is flooded with shit, and it's really gross out here."

I think back to how my mom got furious about small details to cover her more significant problems. If she couldn't afford something, she'd get belligerent about the bank and its systems. That business would give her anything to get her out of there. A plan formulates. I pantomime a phone.

"Yeah, is this casino management?" I shout so Chelsea can hear. "My fucking toilet just backed up in my suite, and it smells like shit everywhere!"

I look through the frosted glass, but I can't see if Chelsea is buying it or not.

"Yeah, you'd better gimme a better room, you son of a bitch," I say. There's nothing but silence from inside the shower. I can feel the anxiety building. I try to hold it down, but I can feel my gag reflex building up.

"Even better than this room?" I shout. "Wow, all right, we'll be right over there!"

Then I hang up the fake phone.

"Did you hear that, darling?" I ask through the door. "They're moving us to a better room! We need to go!"

I crack the shower door carefully so she doesn't see the mess through the door. I peer my eyes inside and see her naked body lying on the shower floor. The water is hitting her legs, and mess is running off her skin in droves. I inch my eyes up her body and catch her arm, poorly wrapped with a scarf. Then I inch up further and find her eyes closed.

"Hey, darling?" I press.

But she doesn't move.

She's fast asleep or dead.

23.

The last thing I remember is an awful smell and my mother laying me gently into a pool of warm water. The water calmed me and cleaned me, and before I could even enjoy its healing power, I slipped right into a dream.

The darkness overcame me and wrapped me up, and it became a large blanket. I felt the blanket mold itself into powerful arms that carried my sleeping body into the sky. I flew and flew, and eventually, I was laid again on that heavenly bed. The warmth overflowed upon me, and I lay peacefully in my dream, never to be disturbed ever again.

After what feels like years of sleep, my eyes gently open, and I see a light. It's blinding at first, but as it lingers, it allows other things to be seen. The tile ceiling above me is ornate and decorated with tiny pieces arranged in an elaborate pattern. The air smells clean, devoid of cigarettes or shit. I take a closer look and find myself in a bathtub half-filled with water. My arm isn't a bleeding cut anymore. It's wrapped intricately with cloth, and my breath is steady. Even though I've lost a lot, I know I'm alive.

My legs and genitals are clean, and I get a good look at all my cuts and bruises. There are so many bruises in certain areas that details can't be made out. I reach my left arm between my legs and feel tremendous, horrible pressure. As my fingers sink below, I locate my asshole and find it burning and torn.

There's a shower curtain hiding the bathroom from the little corner of the bathtub. My fingers shoot out of the water and grip the edge of the tub. I ease it aside and find the plainest looking bathroom anyone has ever seen. It is clean and white and perfect and spotless. There is nothing wrong with it, yet when I look at it, something is wrong with it. I look at it, and it scares me because it's normal. Why isn't there anything wrong with it?

I find myself standing in the water and the water splashing off me and all over the tub and floor. I stand on both feet outside of the bath, then look at the floor, the counter, the grout, the toilet, the ceiling, and the bathtub. I don't understand what I'm seeing. It's a bathroom, but it's not a bathroom. This isn't a bathroom. This is a sinister place. This bathroom is the wrong place, and I'm in danger. Something is coming.

I start screaming and screaming, and I drop to my knees, and my eyes widen. I shout from my gut, and I wail, and I look around, and the walls don't make sense. Why don't the walls make sense? So I scream more. I moan and I wail until the door flings open, and I look up to see a concerned Stacy. I look up at her and cry for help, but I don't know what I need.

There's no saving me from this room. The floor is a spotless white void that I find myself falling into, screaming as I fall. I scream and cry, and Stacy rushes over to comfort me. I don't know what she could do to help me now.

"What's wrong?" she cries.

But then I'm looking into her eyes, and I can't believe what I can see. I look, and her eyes widen and widen and widen until I can see inside them, and all at once, I know that Stacy isn't herself. I scream in her face and push her away as hard as I can with my left hand, and then stand and rush to the corner of the room. I stare down at her, and I'm naked and screaming, and I can't stop. Why am I screaming?

"I'm sorry," she begs. "I'm so sorry."

But I don't know what she's apologizing for.

She's a worm in disguise, just like me.

She's not a human being inside there.

There is no Stacy.

Stacy is the skin suit she wears to make people trust her.

She's everyone's mommy so she can get close, and then

she eats them.

She eats people like a bug with an unhinged mouth.

She's a bug, and she's going to eat me.

"Dahlia!" She starts crying, and then she's overwhelmed, and she's on the ground screaming. She wails and wails and wails, but I don't know what she's screaming about. She screams twice as loud as I scream, and then she overtakes me. I quiet my lungs, and my eyes widen at her. Her gaze cuts through mine like a knife, and I watch as Stacy raises into the sky like a puppet. Her flesh suit is removed. Her skin falls away, and I see the fly underneath.

She arches her neck and back and unhinges her jaw and speaks.

"I never meant to hurt you!" she shrieks. "I always wanted to catch you when you fell."

I stare through the fly and try to find its soul and consciousness, but then I see this disgusting abyss. There's an endless darkness ever-present inside her like a snake. She's a creature that carries the abyss within her.

She looks up at me. Stacy's whispering intensities.

"I killed him. I saw what he did, and I ripped him apart. I ripped him apart like this!" and then Stacy's standing, and with a full fist, she sends her hand through the mirror. It breaks into shards, and the fragments leave gentle cuts on her wrist.

She picks up a piece of glass that's big enough to hold, and in a swift motion, she stabs herself in the shoulder. She screams and screams and screams, and then I'm crying.

"Then I went to Danny's wife's room," she spits, and grabs another shard of glass. "And just like that, there were two."

She plants the glass shard in the same shoulder. The last glass shard catches her hand and tears it open. An extended cut forms down her hand. Its edges part. She screams and then starts laughing. She falls to her knees and laughs and laughs. Then she's crying. She cries and cries.

I hug the corner. I cry and say, "What?"

Her blood leaks through her dress and onto the ground.

The room starts to feel more regular with blood in it. My fear of the room fades and is replaced totally by fear of Stacy.

"I hate myself so much," she cries. She removes the glass shards from her shoulder and throws them across the room at me. I dodge them easily. She's going to kill me.

And right at that moment, there's a knock on the door of the suite. I watch Stacy quickly resume a human shape. Her skin heals, and her blood stops leaking. She stands and grabs a cardigan and tucks her bloody hand in the pocket.

"That's Ethan," she says. "Stay here and compose yourself, then come meet tonight's guest."

She steps out of the doorway and then turns to look back at me. She says, "You'll love him," and departs.

24.

I take my sleeve and carefully wipe the tears away from my eyes and open the door. Ethan is so dashing. He looks up at me from the ground and smiles widely. He's gotta be about thirty, and I've never had someone so young. I don't go for men anymore, which is why this gets to be fun for me. There are no emotional stakes. I won't get attached; I'll just accept the pleasure and say goodbye to the sun. It's getting easier to do.

"Hey there, sweetheart," I hear myself say, and then he leans in and kisses me square on the mouth. I resist at first and then realize that he wants to get right down to it. I honestly prefer that. I open my arms, and he enters them.

"Are you wet?" he asks, and I nod even though I'm not. I can't get my mind off of my beautiful daughter in the other room. I can't help but imagine Ethan being deep inside me as I get ready to make my strike, and then Dahlia's ghost starts wailing from the other room, and he gets spooked and runs away. The only way this works is if Dahlia is here so I can keep an eye on her.

"Ethan, Ethan, Ethan," I mutter, but he pushes me onto the couch. "My daughter is taking a bath in the other room, baby."

And then he stops and sighs. He looks into my eyes with a near frightening intensity and snarls.

"What the fuck?" he spits. "You didn't tell me you had fucking kids."

The irony is that I don't have kids. I've never had kids, and I'm pretty sure that God wouldn't allow me to have kids. I doubt I could even get pregnant if I tried. I just have children. I have my babies I protect and care for, and she's my baby. I consider how I can explain this to Ethan.

"Today's her eighteenth birthday," I hear myself admit. And then I realize there's only one reason I would ever let that slip. I know that there's only one way a man like this will handle that knowledge. I have to lean into it.

"And she's a virgin."

I can see the sweat particles form on his forehead. His mind whirls, and his cock protrudes into my leg.

I have given him a written permission slip to commit a profoundly psychosexual sin.

He could have a mother and daughter.

A mother is a drawback to a guy on her own. But a mother-on-daughter situation could spark something new.

"She's in there taking a bath?" he asks.

"I'm sure she'd love to meet you," I smile.

"I'd sure love to meet her," he smiles.

25.

There's a little gathering of blood on the sink and on the floor, and there's no Stacy. There never was a Stacy. She was a secret fly in disguise. She is looking to lay her eggs. She's going to populate the world with other flies, and they're going to slowly devour the living earth.

But that's not what flies do at all.

Flies help the cycle of life progress.

Flies encourage change and decay and growth and adaptation.

Flies are an essential part of life.

If Stacy is a fly, I have to understand her. She isn't evil; she's trying to do what is in her nature to do.

She is going to help Ethan decay.

She is going to lay her eggs on him. He is going to lay his eggs on her. Together they're going to make a nest of eggs, and then she will kill him. She will help him decay.

So then, what is she going to do with me?

What would a fly want with a girl like me?

I want to live.

I never thought I would ever feel this way about anything.

My mother is a fly. She wants me to grow up to be a fly, just like her.

She's trying to mold me into her.

She wants a partner.

She's lonely.

She needs someone to share in her lifecycle that isn't someone to kill.

She wants me in a way worse than death.

She wants me for life. She wants my life.

She wants to change me into a fly like her.

And then I remember a phrase that wakes me up from this horrible nightmare.

"I can teach you how to like it."

Then I remember the name Lauren.

Lauren wanted to teach me how to like something. I raise my hand to my collarbone and find a bite mark. This was Lauren's first lesson.

Then I realize where I am. This was Lauren's second lesson. I reach my hand between my legs and realize that all my bruises and cuts point to one thing. Then I realize who I am. My name is Dahlia, and I'm no one's daughter. My eyes widen, and I gasp and gasp, and then I see the door slowly opening, and I look down, and I'm naked. I turn and hide my naked body, and then I see a new face.

"Chelsea?" he asks and enters with one step.

The fear wells up in my gut, and I look to the tile ground, and then I know exactly what happened here. I know exactly where I am. I know precisely who Ethan is. It is happening again.

My mind screams and begs God for an exit. I see nothing but suicide. I could grab a piece of glass and end my life before they entered the room and stopped me. I'm already inches from death; I could easily cut my neck and go back to sleep. I remember that beauty sleep.

Then I remember God. The beautiful light that held me so tightly. I looked in the face of her holy light, and she chose me to return. She could have annihilated me, but God protected me because the world is the God that loves me so dearly.

The ground is here to come up and carry me. I was born again to dance on the palm of earth.

I wasn't born to die here.

My purpose. Everything I've decided to live for.

I formulate a plan. The only way out is through. Suicide is giving up. Suicide is easy. Nothing about me is easy.

Nothing will ever be simple for me. I will never choose an easy fate.

I have to enter my darkness.

Ethan enters the room thoroughly, gets a good look at my face, and gazes at my naked breasts. I hide my torn arm just out of sight to attract him. I watch Lauren peek in behind him with a giant shit-eating grin.

"My name is Ethan," he says. "I hear today is your birthday."

26.

Dahlia is splayed out on the ground and hiding her arm like a good girl. I'm worried about her blowing it and killing Ethan immediately or telling him the deal and then making me kill him prematurely. But then I see her controlled expression and know that she's still the woman I love. She's here with me again in the flesh. She's my best friend, just like before. She never left.

My dad always told me you should let things go because they're yours if they return to you. Dahlia came back to me. She came back from the brink of death just to be with me. What was I ever worried about? It's her.

Ethan is so dashing. He walks in the door, and he's an instant charmer. I don't know how he'll react when he sees her arm, and I don't know how he'll react when he sees her dick and her bruises. I imagine all of it will turn him on, and if it doesn't, then Dahlia can help me hold him down.

He approaches with caution but knows what he wants, and he won't hesitate. Dahlia stands her naked body up and hides her dick with her leg and poses.

"Happy birthday!" she says and fakes a laugh. Her eyes dart over to mine, and her eyebrows twist into evil.

She's with me.

She wants me.

She wants to be with me now.

She loves me.

She wants to be with me forever.

We're going to be together forever.

We're a match made in Hell.

Lauren and Dahlia. True love.

I get wet and know what we have to do.

"Y'all have got to be the cutest family I've ever seen," he laughs.

"Chelsea, here is my baby, and I love her with all my heart." I smile and approach her side. I plant a little kiss on her cheek and give Ethan a little wink. I can see him sweating to his core. He's going to melt right out of his clothes, and then he'll just be a little puddle for us to splash around in.

"Aww," Chelsea says and smiles too. "I love you, Momma."

And then, with her left hand, she pushes behind my ear and to the back of my neck. She pulls me forward and kisses me firmly. She pulls my neck tightly to hers, and I feel her wet tongue push between my lips. Then her tongue is stroking mine, and suddenly, I feel weak. I feel a fist reach into my abdomen and grasp at me and pull down, and then a floodgate opens. I want to fuck her so bad. We never got to fuck before she died. I can fuck her right now. I can pull her to the ground, open her legs and fuck her until she loves me again. I want to hear her say it, not for Ethan's ears, but for mine. I want her to tell me she loves me, and I want to see her mean it. I want her to show me how she loves me. I want her to give me her whole life.

Ethan approaches and plants a kiss on my cheek and then moves his lips down. He tries and fails to join his lips with ours and settles for his tongue. He rubs his tongue between both of ours, and they look like little tentacles, and I giggle.

If I take off my dress and cardigan, Ethan will see my wounds, so no matter how much he clings to them, I have to keep them on if I want to lure him all the way in. He tugs at my clothes and practically begs for my nudity with his eyes. I ignore him and pull my sleeve away and run my hand down his body. It distracts him. I can feel the sweat collecting in his hairy belly button.

A man loves to show a woman his cock, not realizing I'm always laughing. My fingers inch down and find a belt. Carefully, I pull at it, and that distracts him. He pulls his cock out, and it's a lot bigger than I expected. I look from his huge

and grips my clit hard with her lips.

I squeal. I yank backward and squeeze my legs. The directness hurts, but I can tolerate it for her. She sucks and pulls, and it's gnarly. I can't enjoy it because it's too hard, but she devours me, and I melt under her tongue. I flex my legs around her head and squeeze. Ethan watches while jerking his cock.

Dahlia sucks and sucks until she's gently biting, and then the hurt turns into a massive, unrewarding pleasure. She gnaws and gnaws, then full-on bites. I recoil and yelp, and she looks up at me with rage. Something in her look scares me, and I quiver inside. My hair stands on end. Here she is, making me nervous again.

Ethan comes up against Dahlia, pushes her out of the way, grabs his cock, and slaps it on my pubic mound. I clench and anticipate the penetration, but only so Dahlia can hate it. I want to see her anger when I take his dick right in front of her. I won't even look at her or show her care if she's going to be a little bitch about it.

I grab Ethan's dick and force it into my vagina. I pull him forward with my legs, and then he's inside me. Dahlia doesn't look with jealousy. She looks around the room and then back at Ethan, then at me, and then at the rest of the room.

"I wanna watch you suck your daughter's dick while I fuck you," Ethan spits and pushes in and out of me. I forgot how much I hate dick. I try to enjoy it, but the unkindness of his approach immediately turns me off. He's not a gentle lover. He's a bastard that likes to cum and get it over with. Dahlia looks resigned.

She inches over to me, and I take her dick between my fingers. It's soft and gentle. She isn't into any of this. I wish there was something I could do to make her love me. I try, and I try, and I try, but she's always thinking about herself. Bitch. She makes me hate her. Why isn't she any fun? Why can't she be fun like me? Why can't she just enjoy shit? Why is she always so distant and miserable?

"Dahlia," I whisper. Ethan looks down, confused, but keeps pushing. "You know I love you with all my heart, right?

143

I've always loved you. I've loved you since the moment I saw you. I knew you were my best friend."

She looks at the floor and tries to hold it together, but I know she can't take much more.

"Baby," I plead. "I want to have a baby with you."

She looks up and gazes into my face, and I grin, knowing I hit the right spot. Just at that moment, Ethan hits the right place, and I contort my body up. I throw my arms around his neck and lift myself. Then I am sitting with him, and then I push him on his back. I put both my hands on his chest and push off to squeeze back down. He sighs from pleasure and tries to keep it in.

I bounce harder and harder, and he straightens out his legs to enjoy every inch of me. Dahlia rushes to my side, and with her left hand, she grabs my arm. She throws her right arm out between us to catch me but finds she doesn't have a hand. Ethan looks up, confused and terrified at Dahlia's injury.

"Don't do that," she says. "I don't want that."

I slam down on Ethan's confused cock, and he looks between us.

"Fuck yeah, Ethan," I wail. "Cum in me. Cum in Mommy."

And he grabs my waist and tries to push Dahlia's injury out of his mind, and then he's pushing and pulling me off his dick. It's getting harder and harder, and I feel every inch of it get warm.

I close my eyes and accept the warmth and push myself down harder and harder, and he pants and pants.

Dahlia leaves my side and stands up. She steps behind Ethan's head and looks into my eyes.

"This is wrong," she says, but then Ethan cums inside me. He wails with euphoria, and I feel the warm jet inside me. I smile and milk out every drop, then I open my eyes and look right at Dahlia.

"I'm sorry," I ask, "what were you saying?"

She picks up a broken piece of glass from the mirror.

27.

I have to live. No matter what. I have to survive. No matter what. So what, I have to suck a dick. So what, I get called demeaning things? I just need to live through this.

Lauren takes his orgasm because she's a fly. She's receiving his eggs so that she may give him hers. She has to populate the Earth with more flies to make everything decay. I pick up the glass shard and stand over Ethan, and I ask myself the worst question an organism ever has to ask: am I a fly too? Can I be like them so I can erase them? Can I really become that horrible to save the whole world from flies?

I inch down to Ethan, and he's still fully orgasming. I push the glass up to his neck, and it immediately chips through some of his convulsing skin. He barely notices from the ecstasy, but then quickly realizes something is up.

"Hey, whoa!" he yelps.

"I should cut off your little dick and make you a tranny too, huh?" I hear myself say, and internally gasp.

"Whoa, okay!" he shouts. He looks up at Lauren for help. But she doesn't offer any; she just sits on his dick and watches the show.

I look at Lauren, and she grins at me approvingly. I throw my look down at him, and his eyes lock with mine.

"I'm sorry," he says. And then I feel the blood running down my hand and realize how hard I'm gripping the glass.

"Kill him," Lauren says and smiles.

He gets uncomfortable with that possibility and starts wiggling. "No, no, no, no, don't."

And then he's pleading with me. "Don't," he says.

I can't. I look into his eyes, and I see the eyes of a savage.

A monster of monsters in this wasteland. But he isn't a fly; he's only the worst of humanity. I can't kill him, so I let him go. I look at Lauren and say, "Kill him yourself."

And then she leans down on him and unhinges herself. Her mouth opens wide, and she bits his chin jokingly. I grab for his arms, and he resists. He gets an arm on Lauren's clothes and rips her off of him in a single motion. Her clothes tear, and her cardigan falls to the floor. She has dried blood all over herself. It's run all down her dress.

I stand and calmly place the glass against my palm with one hand and step back as far as possible. Ethan stands and runs over to Lauren and kicks her in the stomach once, twice. He spits on her. Then he turns and sets his sights on me.

I back up until I find a corner. Ethan approaches with purpose and throws his arms out in front of him. But before he can catch a grip on my shoulders, I drop to my knees and shove the glass deep into his groin.

He doubles backward and falls flat on the tile ground. I approach his jerking and howling body and rip the glass from him. Lauren turns over, groans, then reaches into her breast and produces a folding knife. She unfolds the knife and scoots over to Ethan on the floor.

"You're gonna hurt our baby," she says. She grips his nose with one hand. With the other, she slides the knife across his nose, removing a piece.

He flings his body around and jerks involuntarily. His arms flail up and grab her hair. He rips at her hair, and she screams. I take the glass, and I lean down and stab it hard into his Achilles tendon. He reacts violently, and the glass slips around, cutting my palm but also his heel. He kicks and kicks and kicks. Eventually, the tendon tears, and the glass shard falls to the ground.

He screams and sits up to check the injury. Lauren grabs his face. He turns towards her, and she pushes the knife into his face, and he recoils. He throws his arms up in protest, but I grab one, and she grabs the other, and he falls onto the tile.

Lauren drags the knife deep across his face and makes a massive crease. He stares wide-eyed and horrified as his face falls to pieces. I look at Lauren, and she smiles and says, "It's okay, I think the baby will be okay, Momma," and winks.

He shifts and squeaks and kicks and shakes. I turn to Lauren and know it's happening. This is the moment where she lays her eggs. She accepts his eggs, and then she gives him hers. She wants to provide him with his decay to keep the life cycle moving.

"Baby," she says. "I'm so sorry I fucked up your birthday. I hope this makes it up to you."

She removes the knife from his face and sits on top of him. She lays the knife at my knees and takes his flailing arm from me.

"You can have him," she smiles. "I want you to have him."

I reach down and grip the wet blade between my fingers. My palm is soaked with blood, but I can still hold the grip. I look between the two of them. Ethan screams unendurable bloody murder, but I've heard it before. I listen to it because of Lauren. I listen to it because of the fly. I hold the knife in my hands and get real close to his neck. Then I relax and sit back.

"Thank you," I say, and reach the knife up to my own neck.

As she recoils in fear, he gets a firm grip on her wrists and throws her across the room. He sits up and finds the shard of glass on the ground and jams it into my leg. I recoil and scream out in agony. I look down. The glass sticks directly through my leg. He looks up in pride at finally penetrating me. It's my first stabbing. He's taking my virginity, and he's so proud.

Lauren sits up and huffs before throwing her hair to one side, standing and rushing to Ethan's side. She kicks him in the face with her high heel and he ragdolls. She kicks him again in the side of the head, and it hits the floor. He rolls over onto his back just in time to see Lauren's heel come down and push on the top of his skull. She pushes gently. There's a light crack, and he screams, and his hands are on her heel, and he's pulling her. But she presses, and the heel slides gently from the tiny crack it formed in his skull down to his eye socket. It slides in with no effort.

He screams a final scream, then falls silent when the heel lodges in his brain.

Lauren is panting, and so am I.

28.

"Why do you have to be such a bitch?" She steps towards me. She bends down and rips the glass from my leg. I cringe. The feeling boils me.

"I just want to have fun," she says. "I just want to be happy and love you and have a good time. I want to have a family with you. But you just can't be fun. You can't be anything more than a fucking child."

And then I remember what it's like to be yelled at by my mom. I remember the shame of always being a failure.

"Well, maybe I don't need you anymore!" she shouts. "How about that? How much do you really intend to lose?"

She gets down into my face and pushes the piece of glass up to my nose, and I know she means it. I know she could kill me now if she wanted to. I can't compete with a fly.

"How about I fuck up your pretty little face, so you have something to remember me by?" She's cutting my nose gently, and I'm clenching my whole body with all my might.

"Lauren," I say. She hears her name, and she eases up knowing I said it. She still has a love for me. It's the only thing that can save me now. "We don't have to hurt each other. I want to have a baby with you; I'm just scared. I've never thought about being a mother before. I've barely set out on my own life. I barely even know who I am, and you're asking me to dedicate my life to teaching a little creature all the things that I can't possibly figure out myself."

She eases the glass off my face and relaxes her back.

"I just want to talk about this," she says. "You know?"

"I want to talk about us," I say.

"I love you," she says.

"I love you too," I say.

"How much?" she asks.

"I died for you," I say.

"You came back for me," she says.

"I came back for you," I say.

She lays the glass shard down and sighs.

"When you wouldn't wake up," she says. "I panicked, and I had to bail, and then I came back for you, but you were gone, and I couldn't find you.

"I mourned you, and it hurt me so bad. I did so many horrible things. I'm such a horrible person. I'm a monster. I just didn't know...how to deal with everything without you."

"I thought I was the one that needed you." I smile. She smiles back.

"You don't need me," she laughs. "No one needs me. The world would be better off without people like me in it. I have tried my whole life to fall in love and do something right. I just wanted to be...the best, you know? I wanted to be the best person anyone ever loved. I wanted to show the person I loved the greatest time of their life. I never wanted the person I loved to feel scared of me. I guess I just get scary to protect myself from harm."

I know she's full of shit. I know her now. I know her intimately. I know she is only trying to make herself look innocent.

"You don't scare me at all," I say and touch her bloody hand with my bloody hand.

"You scare me to death," she laughs.

"I don't mean to scare you, Lauren," I say.

"I know," she reassures me. "I just get nervous around you because I think you're the love of my life."

There's a silence between us, and we calmly look at each other. She's a person just like the rest of us. She has a little heart inside her with a bit of desire. It goes beyond the biological need. It goes beyond whatever desires she may have to harm others. She has a little heart with a little love that she made. She made a little love, and she wrote "Dahlia" on that love and called it mine. It's her love to have.

I don't have to share her sentiment. I don't have to share in her love. I am the love of her life, but she's not mine.

I am my own love of my life.

I am my own mother.

I don't need anyone but myself.

I don't need anything anymore.

"You're right," I say. "I don't need you, Lauren."

She processes the words. Something in her knows that this will unravel everything she's built. All the things she did for me. All the things she did to me. No matter what she does, she will never make them have meaning.

"You don't?" she asks.

"No, Lauren," I say. "I need to go home."

"But you don't have a home anymore," she says. "Your home is with me; you killed your mother. You burned her alive."

"I lit a fire in my closet before I left, but I don't think I killed anyone," I say. "I just said that so you'd like me."

"I do like you, Dahlia," she says.

There's another pause, and then I look up at her, and I'm ready for honesty.

"I don't think I like you back, Lauren," I wince.

She lowers her head and cries to herself. She looks up, and she's torn into two pieces.

"Why not?" she begs.

"I don't know," I say. "You really want me to be like you and…I'm not."

"But," she interjects. "You can't possibly know what you want. You can't possibly know that we're bad for each other. Things can change; you can't say that."

"Lauren," I whimper. "I need to go to the hospital."

"You don't know what's good for you, Dahlia!" she shouts. "You don't know what you need!"

"I just need to go to the hospital," I say.

"I'll take care of you!" she shouts. "We don't need to go

anywhere; I can take care of you!"

"No, Lauren," I whisper, and then I feel myself fading away again.

"Dahlia, don't go!" she shouts, but I'm already gone.

29.

I carry her back to the bedroom, and I lay her in bed. She's my angel, and I can't lose her. If I take her to the hospital, she and I will have problems. We need to avoid problems right now; keeping her calm and healthy is the best way. We need to get out of the casino before morning, and I have to pay for another night. We need the clean-up crews to arrive and fix the mess I've made.

This is a mess I've made. I took a young girl's life, and I made it theater for myself. I made her pain my pleasure because it was easier than being me. Ever since I saw her, I knew I had to drag her into my problems. She didn't deserve it, but does anyone? Does anyone ever deserve to get handed someone's whole life's problems? No one deserves it, but we do it all the time with the people that we love. It's an integral part of love.

I caused this angel a lot of trouble, and as I look down on her, I realize that she's very right. She doesn't need me anymore because she never needed me. She didn't need a partner, a guide, a teacher, or anything but someone to hold her hand and tell her everything was okay. I couldn't be that much; I had to be more.

I run to the bathroom to collect my knife, and I hold it to my chest. I lay next to Dahlia in bed, and I fold and unfold the blade. I'm just waiting for her to wake back up. I know any minute she's going to wake up, and she'll be full of energy and love again, and she'll be so happy to see me. I open the knife and clear its edge and look at the reflection I see.

I see myself, and I'm tired. I'm broad in the lens of the

153

knife, but I can make out some of my details. I'm such a disaster now. Today was the worst day of my life. And you know what they say about the worst day of your life: it's usually the last day too.

I contemplate not existing anymore. I am in an endless life cycle of falling in love and then hurting people and then feeling guilty for causing harm, so I jump in bed with another only to break them worse. Now I'm here. Now I'm killing people. Now I'm in the worst imaginable cycle.

I hate myself because I still love Dahlia, and that love gives me too much of a reason to live. I can't ever imagine leaving her behind now, but I know that I'm only causing her pain. When I look at her, I see her elegance and beauty and her radiance and ability to warm up a room, and I want to kill her. She's a perfect miracle. She's the most perfect light that God ever made, and she's mine right now. When she wakes up, she's going to tell me she's had enough and she's going to leave.

I lean on my side, and I grab her left wrist. It's cold to the touch. I place the knife at the base of the wrist, and I look into her face one more time before…

No, she didn't deserve any of this. Look at her. Why would you stamp out light so beautiful? You're just like her mother. You force her to hate you so badly that she wishes you would die. I'm just like my dad. He stamped out my light when I was a kid, and now I get the world back by stamping out beautiful lights. She's a lovely light, and she doesn't deserve to die.

If I want to kill so badly, why don't I kill someone that deserves it? I'm in a casino filled with rooms, and all of them have assholes and bastards in them, and any number of them will do. But how many bastards will it take before I realize who I'm actually trying to kill and what I'm actually trying to do? This has always been suicide, and now I have the knife in my hand, and it's my time.

I could take Dahlia with me, but I like the idea of her joining me one day when she's ready. I wonder what it's like after you die. I wonder if you feel anything. I keep waiting for Dahlia to be my best friend and learn all that I have to teach because I wish someone would do what I do to me. I have always felt like such a coward in the face of death. The idea of losing Dahlia is so much worse. I have such morbid curiosities, but I've never thought to enact them in the most directly observational way.

I look over at Dahlia's torn-off wrist, and I suddenly get jealous. She can't have much time left, and I shouldn't let her go alone.

With the knife open, I grip my left hand against my chest, and I push the blade against my skin. It doesn't go through. I can't force it hard enough on myself. I arch the knife to a point and place it at the crest of my wrist. I pull towards my body as hard as I can, and the knife goes in. I hold back pained cries to let Dahlia sleep.

I force the knife deep into my wrist, and I twist it. I twist and turn until I hear everything break apart, and my wrist is laying loose against my chest. I place my hand under my chin, and with all the effort I have, I yank my arm. Suddenly, I feel a magical sensation overtake me. It feels amazing, and the more I pull, the freer I get. I yank and yank and yank, and then my hand comes off. My wrist explodes with blood and flies across the bed while my hand remains resting under my chin. With my remaining hand, I take it and place it next to me at my side.

The feeling is like nothing I've ever experienced. All at once, I can feel my hand, and then I can't. Suddenly, all my senses are replaced by nothingness. There isn't a hand to hurt anymore. I lie in a state of euphoria. I try to grab things with my missing hand, but my wrist just wriggles and writhes without purpose. I smile, having learned the greatest truth of being alive. It feels better to be nothing than something. Death doesn't hurt.

I take the knife with my left hand and dig it up into my neck. I feel it puncture my vitals, and the blood comes rushing out all over me. I struggle to breathe and know I don't have long, so I rip, and I tear, and I rip, and I tear, and finally, I know I'm going to die.

As I feel my life slipping away, I let loose a tear and embrace Dahlia. I curl my legs around her and I bundle myself up to her for a warmth that I'll never feel.

I turn to look upon the face of the love of my life one last time. I'm so glad I had you. I know I'll never have this baby with her, and I'll never get to see her grow old and raise it and love it. I know I'll never get to feel her hands on my body or her kiss on my face. But even if I stole it, I was happy to have it at all. Thank you for your time and your love.

30.

Light pours in the big bay window, and it's morning. The sun covers my body and fills me with warmth. I can feel another person's skin against mine, but it's chilled to the touch. Nevertheless, my arm is around her and my legs are tied up with hers and I'm in a bed. I slept in a bed for the first time in so long.

I open my eyes, and I see an ornate tile ceiling. My own personal hell is ornate tile ceilings. I passed out at the worst time, and I knew that it would be the end for me as I fell asleep. Yet here I am. I'm awake, and I'm in immeasurable pain.

My whole body feels like a sore on the top of your mouth.

Like a fool, my first concern is Lauren and where she might be and what she might have done to me in the night. I sit up slowly. Then I see her all cuddled up beside me.

She's clinging to a knife with one hand. Her other hand is detached from her body and lying at her side. Her neck is wide open, and her face has a peaceful expression. Lauren is finally dead.

Perhaps she wanted us to be Juliet and Juliet, but here she is, just a corpse. She's bloated and cold to the touch. She's rigid and unmoving, stuck permanently in a cuddle.

I am terrified at the ghastly sight and recoil in shock. Her gore is splayed out so beautifully for all to see, as if she is no longer ashamed of what's inside her. Her peaceful face scares me. Her wounds are deep and putrid, but she has found a peace that I will never long to know again.

In her last moments, she tried to be me and failed. It

drove her to suicide. I drove her to suicide, and all I had to do was not want her anymore.

I fall onto her chest and cry. I hit her chest with my fist as hard as I can, and I cry.

I cry because it's over, but I also cry because even though I never really loved her, she loved me. She loved me with her whole heart, and she let that love destroy her. It killed her and so many others. Maybe they deserved to die, maybe she deserved to die, but she was born to raise hell. She was the last person anyone should ever meet accidentally, and yet I have to thank her.

I'm less human than I've ever been, and yet my fear has turned to resolve. I think I can do this. I think I can make it out of this. I think I can live. I don't want to be her Juliet. I don't want to die with Lauren.

I think I can live without her.

I crawl to the edge of the bed and try standing. It's a challenge because my leg is damaged. I limp my way to the wall, and I lean on it with my left arm. Gently now. Easy. I walk carefully to the front door, and I open it. I stop to give one last look back.

It was Lauren's love, not mine. It was Lauren's show, not mine.

At the last moment, she removed herself from the world to spare me. She made this really easy for me, but I have to carry myself to the finish line. It has to be me now. She can't be my mom, and she shouldn't have ever been.

But I think she would have been proud to watch me walk myself out of this.

I walk out into the hallway, and it's quiet. There's no one but me, and I limp to the elevator and push the button.

If I can just get outside, I know I can make it. Lauren taught me that I can genuinely survive anything. Lauren taught me that I loved myself. I know that when it gets hard, I will crawl out of the dirt to stay alive. Because life is precious and beautiful. It's beautiful for me because I made it myself. No one ever gave it to me. No one ever made it easy. The people I was meant to love only made it harder on me.

But now I'm here, and I'm not scared. I'm the scariest bitch anyone has ever seen. I lost my arm in a grave. I was stabbed in the leg with glass. I am tough as nails, and no one can touch me.

I can protect myself now.

I can be my own mother.

I can take care of my own needs.

I don't need anyone else but me.

The elevator doors open, and I limp out and collapse on the marble ground. Someone rushes over and asks me if I'm okay, and I forget words, and things get so difficult to see.

I know I'm missing my arm at the wrist.

I know my face is bloodied, and I'm covered in so many different fluids. I'm covered in so many fluids from so many people, yet I'm the one that's on the ground. Any moment now, the authorities are going to be here, and a medical team will be here, and the person who buried me and took my arm will be here.

But I don't want to meet that person.

I don't want to know who took my arm. I don't want to know who buried me. None of us ever get that luxury. Why should I?

If I can just stand and get to the door, I know I can do it. So I push the spectators off me, and I pull myself up as much as I can. I crawl to my knees, and then I'm standing, and then I'm limping, and then I'm walking.

I take a step and then another. Through the giant bay window, I can see the sun and it's beautiful today. The sun looks like my lady-god. She's ready to embrace me again, this time for life instead of death. This time, she will greet me with a smile.

And then I walk myself right out the fucking door.

Everyone tries to stop me.

Everyone tells me that I can't take care of myself.

Everyone thinks they know me better than I know myself.

But I know myself, and I know I like the heat on my face. I don't think I ever want to leave it again.

ABOUT THE AUTHOR

Cutting her teeth as a horror film critic on YouTube, May Leitz turned to writing over the Covid pandemic. After reading an indie horror book that left something to be desired, May saw an opportunity to create a work of extreme horror fiction that delivered on both the spectacle and the worldview that helps one deal with the world's darkness. Channeling themes of PTSD and complex situations of abuse, May's first published work, Fluids, is a stream-of-consciousness look at both the violent internalization of a sadistic personality and the vulnerable victim who longs to live for herself. The book was met with indie popularity and some critical success, so May decided to write a second book, taking her time to write something exploring the opposite of the prior work's worldview. Girl Flesh is the byproduct of a year of travel and comfort in the face of strife. The story again follows two clashing personalities coming together to lean on one another in a challenging situation, motivating them to make life-altering changes to promote a happier life together. Her third book, due out later in 2024, titled Rosalind, is what May sees as capping off a trilogy about lesbians under challenging situations and how to manifest the life they want for themselves within the backdrop of extreme horror.

Writing fiction has helped May comprehend the complex events of her life and the bright future she intends to build. Her titles are published through Hear Us Scream Press. She would like to thank her frequent editor, Briar Ripley Page, and her family for tolerating endless nights of pouring over rewrites. May Leitz lives in Colorado with her girlfriend, Laura, and their dog, Gizmo.

www.ingramcontent.com/pod-product-compliance
Ingram Content Group UK Ltd.
Pitfield, Milton Keynes, MK11 3LW, UK
UKHW021936310125
454496UK00013B/696

9 780645 962444